Dancing Star

Creating Déjà vu

A Short Novel by
Don Gunnin

With a multitude of help from
Lee Murray

Text Copyright © 2015 by Don Gunnin

All rights reserved

Prologue

He had said "I was hoping for a lean, classical form with simple action, but replete with rich symbolic gestures and deep theological implications. What I have instead is a ragged figure descending from the high mountains in the person of two voices. One, a formerly blind prophet who, while camping in the Rockies, recovered his sight and to some extent regrets the restored vision, and the other his friend and assistant who in the emerging dialogue becomes a spokesman for the rationally ordered life.

■■■

Between Entreves and Chamonix on route 506, on the road from Torino, there's a tunnel, 7.2 miles long, through the French/Italian Alps. When you exit on the Chamonix side there's an obelisk, a huge monolithic sculpture that travelers stop to photograph and admire. It points away and upward, to Mt. Blanc, or the moon, or perhaps Venus. A German philosopher like Martin Heidegger could have walked the trim pathways around the base, thinking and asking "what is thinking?"

He who is not a German philosopher may still spend the night in Chamonix in a Novatel, and sit outside a sidewalk-cafe the next morning for breakfast, having croissants, marmalade and espresso. He may think about thinking if he wants but it's not necessary.

Chapter One

"The word for abyss is still just another word, and it's the 'still-justness' of the situation that is so preposterous."

****

The right-hand lane of the eastbound Eisenhower Tunnel was blocked by traffic cones while Jesse Gonzales replaced fluorescent tubes from the crow's nest of the Genie Z30 cherry picker. He was about 125 feet from the east exit, and a little surprised that Loveland Basin was blasting for avalanches. Early in the morning before the lifts open, the ski patrol fires mountain artillery into hazardous snow banks above the slopes to pre-empt the potential for skier-caused avalanches. But there hadn't been much snow in the last two days. It had been unusually warm. Half-thinking while replacing the light cover, Jesse supposed the warmth was creating the threat. Another boom sounded as he moved to the next fixture.

On the other end of the tunnel, Howard Brodnax was also replacing tubes. He and Jesse would meet in the middle, checking or replacing several thousand light tubes along the way. At first Howard didn't think much about hearing a boom. He was used to ski area explosions.

But wait! This was the west end of the tunnel. Loveland is on the east. Why would he hear it on this end? It must have been an echo.

Then he heard a rumble -- not of snow but of rocks. What the hell's happening? He lowered the crow's nest and ran the hundred or so feet to the west entrance. Looking up toward Coon Hill, he could see a rock avalanche building and rumbling down toward the tunnel's parking lot. Boulders, some the size of refrigerators, tumbled in an orange dust. A moment earlier these rocks had been as stable as the mountain. Now they had been detached by cascading forces and sent rolling among the tree trunks like volley balls. Large pines, uprooted by the leading edge of the slide, fell across the slope of the hill and slowed the onslaught. The avalanche lost momentum and stopped about 300 yards from the picnic tables. Howard looked back up toward where it began. He thought he saw a white robed human figure dart back over the ridge.

****

The Eisenhower Tunnel crosses the continental divide at 11,112 feet above sea level, about 60 miles east of Denver. North along the spine of the divide, past 500 miles of softly folding white mountain peaks, above barren rocky slopes, alternating with mixed stands of fir, spruce, aspen and pine, past the Bridger-Teton Forest, west of Moran Junction, Wyoming and 6,500 feet just above Jackson Hole, Theodore Boudreaux stood at the edge of camp overlooking Granite Creek.

To Theo, Granite was the definitive mountain campground. There was Spruce over on Slumgullion Pass with a rock formation that the ancestors of the Utes marked as the gods' original form of duck-rabbit, and there was Lodgepole near Glacier on the Canadian border in Montana. But Granite was paradigmatic. Isolated along the Hoback Range, plenty of firewood and water, upper Granite Creek for fishing, an hour's drive to Jackson Hole, hot springs up at the end of the valley for bathing. Truly, a throne for mountain gods who had created the surmounting rock formation, duck-rabbit in name. An optical illusion and a reminder of the fragility of mind, the duck-rabbit was a duck or a rabbit but never both.

Hard as he tried to avoid regimentation, the days were fairly routine. Dawn came late, since the sun had to struggle over Gossett Ridge before imposing its waking command on his lean-to. Crawling out of a sleeping bag, Theo began the day stoking the almost spent coals left over from last night's campfire. Now, at the edge of camp, the gold of aspen leaves made a color coordinated backdrop for a line of yellow piss, sourced from the last night's coffee and Southern Comfort, at that moment streaming within the gray-blue boundary of his legs. The piss entered tiny cracks of the metamorphic rock underfoot to begin its work of freezing, expanding and breaking the ageless rock apart. Theo contributed in his incremental way to the rugged sculpture of the Rocky Mountains.

Philip was still asleep in the lean-to.

No place was as transforming as a camp in the Rockies. No experience or language blended memories of being and time as thoroughly or as mysteriously. Whether it was sight, sound, duration or lighter stimuli that scarcely reached consciousness, such as atmospheric pressure or maybe the oxygen content of the air, Theo frequently tried to give meaning to the disparate bundles of perceptions and metaphors that bent and shaped his thought.

Years ago Theo was a student of logic and philosophy of science at Tulane. He adopted a dualistic mien. Exceptional academic achievement and growing worldliness were compiled with the persona of a kid from Plaquemine, Louisiana who -- like anyone named Theodore, Theophilus or Timothy -- was still called T-Boy. Other students at Tulane saw him as small, dark and unprepossessing, without much campus-life stature but generous and remarkably intelligent when engaged. Like a lot of private people, his inner life was more complex than what was showing on the surface. At times he thought he would reveal his true self to the people of the world or at least to the dark beauties with the soft and familiar Cajun accents that gathered in New Orleans from places like Thibodaux, Choupic, or Labadieville. But then, Theo wasn't sure if his true self was really Louis Pasteur, Samuel Coleridge, Genghis Khan or Popeye so he waited.

His talent for logic and mathematics led him into systems analysis and programming on the leading edge of the computer revolution. He moved to Silicon Valley to associate with other very private revolutionaries. In that glorious dawn of New Age capitalism, he copyrighted a unique graphic visualization of root symbolic logic operations and retired on his residuals.

For five years, he drifted between San Francisco and New York writing poetry. For a programmer, he became a fairly-well-read poet, that is, someone who might sell 2,000 copies of a twenty page book. As a programmer, he wasn't as much analytic as relentless. He didn't rest until he generated all the possible solutions and selected the obvious best. A mathematician like Hardy would say

Theo had the innate ability to see the beauty of a formula as the criteria for its truth. As a poet, his readers considered him inventive and incisive but lacking in conflict. That didn't bother him a lot. A logician's intuition of the uniformity of structure at the base of language inspired a vision of uniform and conflict free communication. He would have discovered how to weave ephemeral syntax dependent meanings together in a context vacuum if such meanings existed. Most recently he was blending European self-consciousness inspired by Rilke with fragments of blues and Cajun lyrics taken from his own polyglot Louisiana heritage. A woman, poet, critic, friend and occasional lover in New York suggested that this style of poetry was too easy for him and that he should try a form that offered more resistance.

Granite was so pristine that thinking was especially easy. In early-October the ground was covered with golden brown aspen leaves thinly frosted with the previous night's dusting of pure white snow. By noon, the snow would melt and the leaves reflected the brilliant fall sun across thousands of gilded surfaces. Camp was in a clearing amid seventy-foot pine and spruce trees on a ridge about twenty feet above Granite Creek. This spot obviously had been chosen sometime in the recent past by elk hunters, who had constructed a makeshift corral for their horses and even built a one-sided outhouse. Activity in a one-sided outhouse was open to scrutiny by most of the world but private when seen from the perspective of the camp.

Theo and Philip Alathon had built their camp there two months earlier. For the past several years -- whenever they could, in the ten years since graduate school at Tulane — they had come for the annual two weeks when the aspens transformed themselves from ordinary biological engines into avatars of ideal beauty, glorious and splendid, beyond practical reason or purpose.

But this year, Philip was blind. He was thirty eight-years-old -- a sculptor -- actually, if he wanted to sell anything on the international art market, he'd call himself a maker of conceptual objects -- a visual artist anyway, who, six months ago, had gone suddenly blind. When Philip entered a hospital in New York for experimental surgery, Theo left a seminar at San Diego State and took the next flight to La Guardia. At the hospital bedside the medical specialists in attendance offered no diagnosis or prospect for recovery.

Theo insisted that he and Philip abandon the specialists to their speculations and make the annual pilgrimage to Granite. On that trip Theo would become Philip's eyes.

A logician who had a bent for poetry could transform the visible scenery into invisible language.

Theo had watched the aspens turn from vigorous lime green to flashing golden recollections of the summer's hard work in photosynthesis. He began describing everything to Philip as best he could but quickly ran out of adjectives, discovering that the spirit of modern poetry excluded much of the language of nature. This was a typical state-of-affairs for metaphor. Fortunately, Granite had good mobile reception. Sometimes Theo would link his phone to poetry archives and get descriptive help from Wordsworth and the daffodils. Late yesterday afternoon, the leading edge of the first fall storm had blown through and began stripping the gray-green aspen limbs of their last bright foliage thus relieving Theo of further need for "gilt, golden, aureus, orchid and tawny" and allowing him to move on to other words.

As the early sun cleared Gossett Ridge beyond the creek it angled through the pine canopy overhead and warmed Theo for a day's worth of renewed camping and describing. He turned back to the camp toward the aroma of chicory coffee and bacon frying. Philip was awake and pouring a cup. He set the blue speckled enamel pot back on the fire, scattering small flames that escaped to oblivion from inside their rock prison inferno. Even in semi-blindness, he had become adept at getting around the campground.

Philip turned his head to the sound of Theo approaching and reached to pour a second cup, "G'morning. Did you sleep well?"

"Well enough, but not much. I promised to upload the last section of Blue Orpheus to Chicago by next week. I was up working on it."

"Is it any good?" Philip's direct questions could get quickly to the substance of something or, just as easily, close a subject by their impertinence.

"It's what I set out to do. If that means anything." Theo located a seat out of the smoke and reached for scrambled eggs.

At the click of a spoon on the tin plate, Philip passed the bacon. It was possible to forget for a moment that he was blind.

Theo had feared that this catastrophe might shatter Phil's world or at least shake up his confidence. But even back in the hospital, Theo had remarked how easily Phil had taken up the challenge of blindness and put aside any obvious concern that the experimental surgery might fail. Taking a deep breath of the fall air, Philip asked, "What time of year do I smell?"

"Brown and green mostly." Theo took a sip of his coffee. "We've been here two months, if that's what you're asking."

After a pause, Theo continued "I wonder if they're thinking about me back down the mountain. If I never returned would the deprived flatlanders sense the power in my absence? Would they look for the cabala of my lost prophecies in those childish love letters to Jan -- remember Jan? – boy, I wrote the most awful nonsense to her -- or my old grocery lists? What scraps did I leave behind that could show them how to reassemble me?"

"If you gave them your e-mail address they could write you for advice from up here."

"There's something about technology that cheapens prophesy."

That morning, Philip was back at his usual spot by the campfire. In a timeless memory swirl, that instant blended evenly with days from the summer of their second year at Tulane.

Then, Theo and Philip had spent eight weeks randomly traversing the Continental Divide from New Mexico to Canada in an old orange Ford van. They had been joined on that trip, and many of the subsequent ones, by Michael Lovell. Michael was a pre-law student who had taken Philip's ethics class as an elective. He had said a lawyer should know where ethics were hidden so he could stay away from them.

That was a thinking trip, or at least a trip which awakened souls and made thought possible. The campfire at Granite, in the opening of a clearing in the trees, became the key piece in the fragmented mosaic which was their collective memory of the trip. They learned that cold night air pushed down the valley in the evenings and that warm air pulled back up during the day. So they went through the twice daily ritual of repositioning their "rock chairs" on the downwind side of the fire. Just before dusk, they gathered enough new firewood to last through the night and morning breakfast. They built tables out of small branches and binder's twine, poured water through a coffee filter held over a speckled enamel pot by a forked branch and talked about the future of philosophy and art.

Theo and Philip were cocky, as graduate philosophy students might be, full of last semester's insights into Plato's Symposium or Blake's Urizen. Their friend and fellow student, Michael, as a pre-law student, wasn't convinced that their flights of speculation, as entertaining as they were, had any practical merit -- mostly he opined they weren't worth any money.

Philip thought the clearing around the campfire was more than just a place to sit without getting brambles up his pants-leg. He said, "If Heidegger were with us he'd call this clearing "clearedness" -- that would be 'lichtung' in German -- and probably go on to relate it to openness. He'd call that 'offen.'"

Michael, said, "Offen could be a circumvention of federal financial institution regulations and Lichtung a brilliant legal strategy worth a fortune to the right lawyer in court."

Theo was getting a bit drunk and started out to say, "Lichtung could just as well defend a dog licking his ass." but curbed the direction of his thought and concluded, "And you mean 'open' as in 'open narrative structure' or 'open grave'? A hole, beckoning for new interpretation or a missing occupant?"

And so on it went. They bantered for hours trying to eliminate the praxis inherent in 20th century language of science and practiced truly encountering things by stripping them of all language driven predisposition. They asked about anticipation in the face of which 'care' was possible. They tried to see something 'as if for the first time' and say 'truly it is so.' They wondered if any progress in thought was possible and allowed Philip to come to his usual conclusion, "Only in poetic language, in metaphor."

One night around the campfire Theo began reading a passage from Camus' Myth of Sisyphus aloud. Philip gazed into the fire, murmuring. Michael dozed over his Comfort and coffee. "And here are trees and I know their gnarled surface, and water and I feel its taste. These scents of grass and stars at night, certain evenings when the heart relaxes --.... You describe it to me and you teach me to classify it. You enumerate its laws.... ...you teach me that this wondrous and multi-colored universe can be reduced to the atom and that the atom itself can be reduced to the electron. All this is good and I wait for you to continue. But you tell me of an invisible planetary system in which electrons gravitate around a nucleus. You explain this world to me with an image. I realize then that you have been reduced to poetry.... So that science that was to teach me everything ends up in a hypothesis, that lucidity founders in metaphor, that uncertainty is resolved in a work of art."

Rife with stoned delusions around the campfire, over yet more coffee and Southern Comfort, they continued long discussions of being and nothingness, art and metaphor, money and law, money and nothingness, art and law, metaphor and being, law and nothingness, art and money and so forth which ended when the Comfort overwhelmed the coffee.

At Tulane, Philip had been a graduate student and teaching assistant in philosophy. Then, fatefully, while preparing to teach a course in aesthetics, he read The Birth of Tragedy again. Nietzsche reminded him that an academic philosopher was an analyzer and classifier of experience. An Alexandrine. A librarian. A file clerk of the soul who knew only how to store and retrieve the dead metaphors, figures and tropes that had become so worn and familiar that they were mistaken for truth. Philip read again that knowledge was not to be found in these exhausted truths but in the affirmation of life emerging in new forms, the created entities -- determined lies in Nietzsche's dark hyperbole -- that were the everyday affairs of art.

As affirmation of life, art is worth more than truth. This bit of Nietzsche's thought, which Philip had known only as a theory and a chapter in the history of philosophy, removed itself from the book shelf and relocated to the center of his own quest for a worthwhile life. Until that instant he hadn't known he was on a quest but now there was no getting around it. So, like the itinerant Cynics, he set out with his satchel, staff, and double cloak, without fear or desire, to journey the wild roads and hazardous byways linking rare points of civilization across a terrible and terrified American continent.

Actually, after failing to convince his professors that a dissertation should rightfully be written in metaphor, Philip took the bus to Kansas City and enrolled in an art school. He raised the faded black banner of anarchy on the banks of the Missouri River.

Philip was born too late to be part of The Movement. His class was old when it was young. The end of a student generation past its prime and out of date. He had missed the chance to lock his professors out of their classrooms until they promised to teach a relevant curriculum or throw rocks at the National Guard when they came to restore the hegemony of irrelevance. Now, as an artist, he would wage bloody revolution at the level of symbolism. Bombs that had only rattled the porcelain in the restrooms of campus ROTC buildings, would explode murderously in the main halls of the oppressive cultural superstructure.

Philip assaulted the hierarchies of common sense. He did violence to the minions of logic. He ripped open and exposed the duplicity of denotation. He was a terrorist in the pleasure gardens of semiotics.

In the school's art curriculum, Philip's discipline was still called sculpture, but his work was more likely to be an offal and excrement-filled moat barring entrance to the school's art gallery -- or sacks of shredded pigeons fastened to perplexing machines that looked like they might drop, throw or otherwise distribute the pigeon parts at any instant. That kind of thing was called conceptual art or performance art but some of the faculty wanted to call it vandalism. Some of the students wanted to know what had taken the lives of the pigeons. The more delicate souls on campus saw him as dark tempered, manic-depressive and possibly dangerous.

But the quest had kindled a nearly supernatural fire in his dark grey eyes which he stoked regularly with amphetamines. Fires of that sort are often attractive to disaffected youth despite an ironic humor, and could be insulting to someone who was paying attention.

Nonetheless, he attracted and small devoted following. Thin, pale, female art students with deep eyes, who dressed in black and talked often of suicide or the higher spirituality of lesbian sex, were nonetheless delighted to discover a trace of life and the temporary allure of heterosexuality in the surprising strength of his slender hands. Strength, which moved big hunks of machinery into radical juxtapositions was balanced with a subtlety that wove fine wire into delicate patterns and new pathways for electrical energy. A muscular, controlled body that wielded a sledge hammer as deftly as a needle made Philip's bed at the rear of his cluttered studio a popular stopover for young women on the way to more durable relationships with less difficult men.

After leaving college his constructions became larger and more complex. He never seemed to have the skill to get anything for himself, but he could always find help for a project. The charisma in his physical exuberance, animated gestures and deep voice could quickly attract a team of supporters. That team might just as easily be dispersed by his impertinence and arrogance. He placed his machines on rooftops, in vacant lots or wherever he could appropriate an empty space for a few hours. The machine would destroy itself in a short length of time whether it was designed that way or not. He always risked charges of trespass, vandalism, or creating a nuisance.

The critical community began to take notice. Some Mid-Western writers, who were fading observers of modernism, said he was foregrounding the essence of technology. More cutting edge, post-structuralist writers with a national readership said he was deconstructing the text of technology. His name was known around but it was a few years before he was invited to show at major museums. Philip's work was always more popular among people who didn't have to clean up the pigeons. Small grants and commissioned performances made it possible for his creations to become even more kinetic, unpredictable and public, leading to an almost inevitable disaster. During the predictable, ensuing lawsuit his eyesight failed.

But in Granite, on a chilly October afternoon, Philip and Theo were crossing the rutted dirt road toward the meadow to the west of the campsite where public creations and disaster were the furthest things from thought. At the distant ridge of low foot hills, a brown line of receding elk flickered for an instant and disappeared. Theo gathered his descriptive powers to paint a word picture of elk tails in a gray haze but Philip interrupted his effort, "T-Boy, I have a great debt to pay."

For a moment Theo thought Philip was about to offer thanks for watching out for him but quickly disposed of the thought. He knew that Philip was completely dependent on him but would never express gratitude with more than a passing gesture. Philip expected Theo to help as much or as little as he wanted. If Theo were leaving the next day, Phil might ask to be guided back into town or he might just say good-bye and find his own way. Theo believed that Phil would sit down on the forest floor and starve to death before crying out for help and that meant Theo could walk away anytime without fear of reproach. Philip believed that the boundary between life and death was very thin and hardly worth thinking about.

Walking out on the meadow into the sunlight, Philip continued, "I think I'll give a gift to this land where we've sojourned so often and so fortunately."

Theo would never have characterized Philip's work as a gift.

Philip elaborated, "I've never given a gift. I knocked out pieces of reality. I expected people would work out for themselves what they could get out of a new look at things." He paused to roll another Bull Durham cigarette in his yellow-stained fingers.

Theo walked a step or two ahead and turned back, "What could I see through a hole in reality?"

Knowing the path from the direction of Theo's voice, Philip took a quick step to catch up and they continued slowly. "I had science backing up my aesthetics. The timing of electro-chemical events in the brain results in patterns -- it's been called bundling -- of sense experience. When those patterns become stable, experience becomes general rather than specific. If I could disrupt part of a pattern, experiences in that bundle would be more specific -- more concrete -- more alive and at the same time more metaphorical. That would mean an increase in consciousness wouldn't it."

"That sounds modern enough. The concrete individual is more real than the coherent abstraction. An ambiguous narrative filled with disconnected events is closer to the truth than a well-made story. Where does that leave metaphor? I've listened to you talk about metaphor till blood has run out of my ears."

"That's what I'm talking about now. I've drifted. Blindness has meshed a lot of my senses back together. I want to try putting some pieces in, instead of taking them out. To build relationships -- metaphorically -- if you don't mind my saying it again. I'll call this a gift. I'll have to think what that means."

Philip paused reflectively. He smiled the smile of conviction and purpose. Theo knew from long experience that a new project was coming on, with a unique set of difficulties for Phil and everyone around him. He was not disappointed. Philip said, "Of course, I'll need your eyes more than ever before. Your descriptions will have to be perfectly clear."

Theo's tablet and design app were always in his pocket. A few touches and gestures brought a universe of romantic description onto the screen. "What do you think of this?" He read one of his marked passages, "With distant prospect among gleams of sky and clouds, and intermingled mountain tops, in one inseparable glory clad, creatures of one ethereal substance, met in consistory, like a diadem or crown of burning Seraphs, as they sit in the Empyrean?"

Philip pondered the quotation for a moment and replied, "I haven't understood a thing you've said since you started reading that damn Wordsworth."

"It was good of you not to be critical."

"Blindness has taught me patience."

Theo remained Philip's friend while most everyone else was eventually pushed away from friendship into awe -- or worse -- by his mysterious self-absorption. Theo had a high tolerance for eccentricity. He knew that everyone wears a mask of some kind. He usually had a guess at what was behind that mask but didn't give it a lot of weight. He had low expectations of humanity in general and little need for conventional courtesy but Philip had succeeded in annoying him. "Blindness asn't taught you consideration. You've let me waste a lot of my time."

"It was your time and still is."

Theo didn't stay annoyed for long, "I came out here to describe aspen leaves and elk butts for my blind friend -- who is grateful I'm sure -- and find myself in a lost episode of Kung Fu."

Adopting a mocking oriental accent Theo said, "Master Po, I have so little time and so much to learn. So, Grasshopper, you think because time has passed it has gone away? Yes master. But where would time be where there was not time? Nowhere master. So is nowhere somewhere in time then? No it is not master. Then time is not lost if it is only elsewhere. I see clearly now master."

Theo had come to know Phil as a conceptual artist, not a watcher or a describer. Phil had not been a connoisseur at life's great banquet of disinterested experiences. He wanted his hands on materials. He wanted to know by contact what he could make a material do or how a process, or a machine could be subverted and redirected from its original purpose. That's why he was missing part of a little finger on his left hand. Some things were not meant to be handled.

Philip picked up the pace. By sound and an occasional brush against Theo's elbow he was guided but kept the appearance of independence. "A little raw honesty shouldn't hurt," he said.

Grabbing Philip's arm just in time to lead him around a puddle, Theo admonished, "Watch your step Diogenes or you'll find yourself honestly wet and muddy."

"I have become that Greek lamplighter. I was looking up to the heavens but fell in a hole. How quickly the messenger is reminded of the difference between heaven and earth."

"The messenger is mortal but his word is god in the love letters to Jan."

"I shouldn't have told you about that. I've not even come close to tapping the last reserves of my will."

Theo set Philip on a secure path and let go of his arm. "It hasn't occurred to me that you might have reached the end of your will." They had never discussed the possibility that Philip's blindness could be permanent.

Philip said, "The western end of Eisenhower Tunnel needs a work. And I'm going to give something to these Rockies. That will be my gift. At the point where travelers emerge from darkness into light -- into the clearing."

"It's not dark in that tunnel. There are thousands of florescent lights."

"That's manufactured light. I'm talking about a gift of the real stuff. It won't be easy -- giving the gift. I can imagine lots of bureaucracies -- local, state and federal -- whose acquiescence is needed. And there's the cost -- construction cost and on-going maintenance."

That made Theo reflective, "I've never known you to think of easements. I don't think you've ever designed anything that stayed together long enough to need maintenance. Like you said, this is going to be new. I bet that's where I come in."

"Maybe, maybe not," Philip replied quickly. He had been thinking about the project for a while. "We could hire Michael. He did as well as anyone could with my lawsuit."

"He did as well as anyone, considering the thoughtless affront of his client to the jury."

"I was sworn to tell the truth."

"Would it be possible that Michael has had as much of your problems as he can stand for a while. He gave you months of work on your case and lost. Not good for his standing in the firm, pocketbook or ego."

"It would be his decision. Maybe Michael would like to come out here and deal with this."

"Deal with what?"They walked on in silence.
****

Michael Lovell worked on Wall Street. He had visited Philip in the hospital in New York daily. For Michael, things always seemed to come easy. His six-foot-two frame was coupled with the air of confidence that comes from excelling in athletics back in Texas where football was a religion. A slightly large nose humanized his appearance a bit and might have kept him from being tempted into a career in on the stage. He was easy-going and the folks in Lubbock said he could charm the diamonds off a rattlesnake. His thick, dark black hair, beard and blue eyes could always make the South Louisiana girls exclaim, "Ohoo, he give me the frisson". Ultimately, his good-nature and innate confidence made people trust him without thinking too much about it. That directed him into a career in law.

After graduating, Michael was admitted to Harvard Law School even though his entrance exam scores were not spectacular. He had put himself through college by starting a business that salvaged electronic components used in oil exploration. Harvard didn't want its entire freshmen class to be just the country's top apple polishers or test takers and so rewarded that kind of initiative intermittently.

Theodore kept in touch with Michael from New York. Once in Cambridge Michael told him, "Now that I'm here I can polish enough apples and ace enough tests to get to Wall Street."

On Wall Street, Michael said, "I can work twelve to sixteen hours a day on tax shelters and limited partnerships and bill more than a few million dollars a year."

Over the next five years Michael learned how to work eight or nine hours a day and bill twelve. He established his contacts, invested his money and left the firm. He said, "I'm making less money on my own, but the air of New York is a lot sweeter when I'm not kissing as much ass."

Michael never admitted much understanding of Philip's way of life but he was always around to listen and help. That was another gap between word and deed that an astute observer like Theo might have reconciled if he cared to.

Philip and Theo hiked all the way down to Lem's Granite Gap Store, which was about a half-hour away. Philip was totally enveloped in thought. Back up near the campsite, the Granite River slowly meandered, wending its serpentine way through the meadow. But as they followed the river on down-valley, the grade was steeper and the river suddenly became a series of mini-cataracts, cascading around boulders which were placed there thousands of years ago by glaciation. As they approached Lem's, the grade flattened out again, and the river crept under a footbridge and flowed into the larger, Hoback River which itself would flow into the great Snake River about 30 miles west. A few hundred feet from Lem's, Theo finally asked, "Want me to call Michael?"

"Yeah, I think it's time.

****

The beach was closed again. A disastrous hurricane missed Acapulco by 350 miles but came close enough to force billions of jellyfish to seek protection along the pristine beaches. Beach alerts became a daily nuisance. Finally, fearing the economic consequences of modern and rich mammalian tourists coming in contact with primitive hydrozoans, the Ministry of Tourism imposed a temporary beach quarantine.

So Michael Lovell decided to tool around Market Centrale rather than spend another day drinking mimosas in the Princess' courtyard of pools.

He wasn't sure what Felicity had planned for the day. Down in Acapulco in the sunshine, away from the daily routine, she was happy on her own. Back in New York she was beginning to demand more attention. She was expecting him to spend more time with the kids, think of his family in front of his daily billings, etc., etc., etc.

Vis-à-vis Felicity, Michael was mindful of the Lucy Fitch Syndrome. He had known Joe Fitch since law school and they were friends in New York. Joe had been a better student than Michael and was even more ambitious. At Lebowitz, Howard, Finkel and Stern, Joe was on a track to make partner in 10 years. He would have been a multi-millionaire in 5 and retired at 55, wealthy and successful. Out ahead of him, Joe envisioned a great life that would begin at 55. He wanted a life that began at 30. His wife Lucy, who had whined and sulked when he worked evenings to put himself through law school, who complained when he wasn't around when she was making the home that they bought on his associates salary, who was heart-broken when he was late for the birth of their second child because a slow contract negotiation had left him snowed-in at O'Hare, was shocked and outraged when he told her he was going to give up his $1,000,000 a year to open a bait shop in Connecticut. So she divorced him.

Even with Lucy Fitch as an example, Michael had been about as successful at changing Felicity's perspective as she at changing his. No doubt he was consumed by work -- that's what brought in the money she spent in the little boutiques in the East Village or art galleries in Soho. Felicity had an eye for quality things and her family's expensive taste. Sometimes she had an heiress' imperfect understanding of where money comes from. Michael was the wellspring of profit and fortune that paid the mortgage on the condo in Lincoln Park, the private schools, the maids, the cars.

But the wealth from Michael's life-giving fountain was never enough. In his mind, Felicity always wanted his thank-god-still-impenetrable soul too. For Michael, It would be reasonable to think that one's soul is his last fortress.

As he prepared to go into town, Michael wondered if the Mexican porters were spending enough time with their wives. But a porter's wife would know, if he came home late, that he hadn't been restructuring a leveraged buyout for Avariceco. She'd know he was getting a bed-making lesson from one of the maids.

Since they had married, Michael was never made in any bed but Felicity's. All of their lifestyle arguments ended in an impasse superseded by pure lust. She was forever the coquettish, seductive Felicity. Finest body he'd ever seen, best love he'd ever had, most beautiful woman he'd ever known. And he had to grant her that she'd always known how to plant a memory in that impenetrable soul that kept him satisfied when he was away from her.

"In the end it's worth it, isn't it?" Michael said out loud and laughed at the unintentional pun as he gave his key to the concierge. The concierge laughed too. Laughing at meaningless jokes is part of the service.

"Oh, Mr. Lovell," the brown-skinned Princess porter yelled just as Michael passed through the lobby to grab the cab, "there's a message for you."

"Who in the world could that be?" he mumbled to himself and returned to the desk for the message.

It was a fax from Sharron. After six years as his paralegal, Sharon had learned how rare and precious vacations were for him -- and for Felicity. But she knew what was important and what wasn't. He opened the fax expecting an emergency. It said Theo Boudreaux had called from Wyoming and needed help with government regulations on a project in Colorado. "Sorry to bother you, Sharon concluded, "but because it's about Philip Alathon, I thought you might want to respond."

Tipping the porter $5, Michael put the fax in his shirt pocket, got in the cab and headed toward the market. It said he could get in touch with Theo and Phil through Lem at the Granite Gap Store. But government regulations didn't seem like much of an emergency.

It had been more than two years since Phil's court case -- one of the few Michael ever lost. Phil's mechanical installation at the Contemporary Art Museum in Cincinnati had broken through a wall and fatally injured an art patron. For a while it appeared as if he is going to be charged with reckless endangerment but in the end it came down to a gargantuan insurance claim against the museum. Michael defended Philip against the museum's contention that he had violated the terms of their agreement with a machine that not only looked dangerous but was dangerous. Philip was judged responsible but impecunious and the museum still had to pay.

The controversy made Philip Alathon an international celebrity. He was condemned from the floor of Congress. The senator from North Carolina demanded that any National Endowment support for the Cincinnati museum be suspended pending investigation. Television and newspaper commentators branded him an irresponsible sociopath and possibly a murderer.

But Philip had his supporters. Many leading artists and critics countered that a mistake is not a crime and radical bloggers suggested that the life of single museum visitor was little price to pay in a war against the repressive ideology and complicity inherent in a contrived language of order and responsibility.

Philip's enemies used shorter arguments and tended to attract more popular backing. He had assumed his usual pose of angry defiance and indifference to any theory that was expressed in words rather than deeds. Then his eyesight began to fail. Michael assumed it was psychosomatic. Philip must have punished himself with a carnal metaphor for failure and guilt.

But later a specialist in New York suggested a possibly temporary physical cause of Philip blindness. That could mean that Philip felt less guilt than Michael would have expected. Perhaps Philip's egotistical pose wasn't a mask and he was, in fact, indifferent to the suffering that his art experiment had caused.

The cab driver turned around, grunting something interpretable as, "where to going?"

Coming out of the semi-seclusion of the Princess drive onto a teeth- clashing, potholed thoroughfare and turning left, the cab went west along the beach road into town. Off in the distance, to the left, streaks of color on the white sand, like an impressionist painting, became on reflection and interpretation, minute figures of people basking in the sun or defying the quarantine and running to and from the edge of the surf, sharing the murky water with the jellyfish. To the right, through the cracked cab window, Michael could make out several mansions overlooking Acapulco Bay, hanging precariously on the hillside, defying gravity and flouting their uncertain future at the top of a crumbling social order.

Michael pulled out the fax and read it again. Philip Alathon and a sculpture in Colorado were, spiritually, about as far removed from Wall Street as a person, place or thing could be. He'd know Phil for fifteen years. He had taken a history of ethics class from Phil at Tulane. To Michael, it seemed that a lot of the time Phil was not trying to be understood or was trying to not be understood. Michael decided he'd call Theo from a payphone at Market Centrale.

Passing through a district of Acapulco where increasing poverty and ignorance seemed inconsistent with heavier motor traffic and energetic trade, the cab finally approached the Acapulco Central Market.

"Let me out here," Michael said to the cabby, "I'll walk the rest of the way."

Grunting something uninterpretable, the cabby threw on the brakes and screeched to a halt. Michael tossed eight dollars in the front seat. Pushing out on the door as he pulled in on the door handle, Michael was gratified that he somehow ended up on the outside of the cab with both feet on the ground. He would follow the canals toward the market and probably run across a telephone station along the way. "Government relations. Colorado." he mused. "What could Philip be up to now?"

He walked a block or so, always amazed that there were men -- boys really -- standing in the seclusion of shadowed alleyways, rifles strapped to their shoulders. In a lively place like Acapulco one could overlook the tension between Mexico's upper and lower classes. The middle class was dissolving away. The government called itself socialist but that just meant an additional privileged class of bureaucrats was grafted onto the usual privileges of wealth. In their dark Mezo-Indian features these soldiers reflected their roots in Mexico's poorest families. Michael wondered which side they would fight on in the next revolution.

Up ahead a telephone symbol pointed to a long distance station. As he approached, he briefly considered passing on by without making the call. After all, he was on holiday with Felicity. He knew from experience that what's important for Philip isn't necessarily important in the global sense. For Philip, everything relating to him was important. But turning over in his mind the legal puzzles that Philip might be sending his way, Michael realized that he was getting bored watching the thong bikini's strolling the paths among the interconnected pools and gardens of the Princess. He hadn't talked to Philip since he left the hospital in New York. There was an empty booth at the telephone station, so he figured, "what the hell."

He pulled the fax from his pocket, picked up the phone, and directed the operator to call the number. "Si" he responded as she instructed him to hang up the phone and then pick it up again when it rang. It was a little after three p.m. in Acapulco, two o'clock in Wyoming. In about five minutes the phone rang and Lem was on the line. The connection was fuzzy but Michael was able to make Lem understand that he was in Acapulco and would return to New York in two days. Could he let Theo and Phil know they can contact him after that? Lem said he'd get the message to Philip and Theo.

Michael hung up the phone, gave his Visa Card number to the señorita who placed the call for him, returned her smile and walked out onto the plaza at the edge of the Market. His gut told him it was time to get back to business. Sun and sex with Felicity was par excellence. Yet after three-plus days of working at relaxing, he was tired of it. Any further effort at refreshment would have diminishing returns on investment.

Absentmindedly, he wandered through the Market. The aroma of fresh fish and vegetables was interrupted every so often by a whiff of stagnancy or decay. The smell of blood from the open meat markets excited vague, primitive appetites for the taste of a fresh kill but the sight of flies having the times of their lives partying on animal carcasses brought him back to an appreciation of government inspected, plastic wrapped beef back in the USA.

He lingered at the stall of a marionette retailer. Most of the puppets for sale were simple ceramic heads on cloth bodies but, to attract a clientele, the proprietor was manipulating a tiny ballet dancer with a dozen strings. It was a very professional performance.

Felicity had taken him to a performance by a puppet theater in New York. It was a kind of show called Bunraku with three Japanese guys working the different parts of a rod puppet. They didn't try to hide from the audience although the underling puppeteer who worked the feet had to wear a black hood so he wouldn't distract from the main guy who was working the head and right hand. Felicity was fascinated. She collected puppets and scale models. She was drawn to miniature worlds. In a sense she lived in a miniature world of fashion, art and literate conversations with other extremely well-educated and well-cared-for women. Michael was impatient -- in fact quite irritated -- by a mechanically adroit but essentially lifeless puppet show. Much of what was new and interesting in Felicity's world appeared to Michael as nothing but a talent for formal innovation executed without content or purpose.

Michael often questioned how their east coast intellectualism and rough Texas pragmatism had managed to mesh. It must have had something to do with money and sex. Universal solvents.

Michael looked over the marionettes for one to complement Felicity's collection of Indonesian dancers and Balinese shadow puppets. He knew that Felicity was too politically correct to be comfortable owning a Mexican bandit. Someone in her social circle was bound to consider that a racial stereotype. So he bought her a brightly colored washer woman. A puppet with a laundry basket could be displayed guilt free as long as it was understood that the woman was washing her own clothes and not the clothes of an Anglo exploiter. It was also inexpensive enough to be discarded if the political context changed.

With this small bundle under his arm Michael moved aimlessly through the crowd, thoughts turning again to Philip Alathon. Philip believed that the more insoluble and irritating, an intellectual dialogue became, the more value it had. He believed in judgement delayed and problematized. Michael held that the point where theoretics become intellectually irritating the thinker would, of necessity, either shit or get off the pot. Philip had a moral investment his self-defined marginal status and relished his gadfly posture. Michael wouldn't have been surprised to see him coming down the halls at Tulane wearing the tattered robes of Socrates -- or Jesus -- as if poverty was a necessary and sufficient condition of thought. At this point in the dialogue, Michael always decided to get off the theoretical pot and onto the practical pot of law, where a shit at least had content. Like Michael's coach back in Lubbock who was only about five feet tall but would get after some big old linebacker, bellowing, "You think you can fuck with me boy!" He'd get a hold of the startled player's jersey and be right in his helmet screaming, "You think my shit don't stink!" and be spitting all in his face. That was content.

Actions that were from the heart and had the drive for economic-well-being were real and didn't need a lot of theory to hold them up. Michael quoted from something he had written early in his life when he thought he might become a writer. He recited out loud, unheard and ignored in the din of the market crowd, "The somnambulist said, all too often, speech, while defining the project extinguish the prospect. The somnambulist must go on dreaming lest he fall."

Flashes of memory can fill long intervals of time. In one brief memory were bundles of symbolic logic, football practice and Nietzsche, then Philip

Alathon and Theo leading to campsites and mountain vistas, then the intellectual Felicity, always followed in close consort by the hot Felicity, Bunraku, Southern Comfort, and campfires. Thoughts blocked out the other senses. The past supplanted the present.

Without conscious direction Michael had walked to the curb on the south edge of the market where a cab was waiting.

Somnambulantly, he got in the back seat and directed the cabby to the Princess. He knew he was ready to leave. It was late afternoon. Another gorgeous sun's customary orange seduction of a purple horizon was being pursued off to the west accompanied by a chorus of serenading seabirds. It was boring. Michael missed the brown air and cacophonous racket of New York. He got his key at the front desk -- no messages -- and headed up the staircase to their suite.

Felicity was out on the balcony watching the kids swimming in the pool below, doing her toenails. "Hi Babe, glad you're back." She was just as fresh after a day's hard shopping as first thing in the morning. Amazing. She said, "Let's have some caviar and champagne and enjoy the night before we think about heading back home. OK?"

She was fuckin' amazing. She knew that four days was all he could take. She probably knew before he did that he was bored.

"You're the wisest woman in the world, Felicity. Did anyone ever tell you that?"

"You've told me a million times, and I've loved it every time. I'll cut your tongue out if you stop saying it." Only a woman of Felicity's quality could threaten symbolic castration in such a generous and loving way. "Anyway, regardless of my virtues, you're the most stimulating man in the world. Did I ever tell you that?"

"No, never. This is news -- great news -- to me. I always thought you thought I was a complete bore."

"You are. But I love you anyway. Will you call room service?"

Michael went to the phone, knowing he was about to be seduced again by the only woman he'd ever let get close to him. He called room service for some Beluga and Dom Perignon, went to the vanity, splashed some water on his face, and returned to the balcony.

"Sharon sent me a message from Theo Boudreaux about Philip."

Felicity's voice was concerned, "Is he OK?"

"Yeah. There wasn't anything about his health. They're up at Granite. It's a campground in Wyoming. I've told you about it before. Philip wants to put a sculpture in Colorado. They want me to help them through some bureaucratic maze regarding its location."

"I bet they want it free. What are you getting into?"

"I'm not sure but it should be interesting."

Felicity stiffened, "At least as interesting as the lawsuit by the museum."

"I'm a lawyer. I helped out a friend who was going to court."

"And when you need help building a machine that will tear up your office and kill you, he'll be there for you."

"Philip thinks differently from other people."

"But what about your reputation? Criminal lawyers have to associate with murders, rapists and extortionists. The more hideous the criminal the higher the reputation of the lawyer that gets him off.

But you're in corporate law. Doesn't it matter to your clients?"

"I don't think so," he said weakly. Felicity liked Philip Alathon well enough. He could actually be charming when he had to. But over the years, Michael had noticed a hidden reservoir of resentment of Philip that bordered on jealousy. He tried not to tap it that afternoon. "Yeah, but what the hell." Michael's defensiveness flowed momentarily, then after a couple of seconds, ebbed.

"Come on Fel. Old campmates have to stick together."

"They have to grow up eventually," Felicity said with the beginning of a smile. She was also trying to keep this discussion from turning into an argument.

"I don't know. T-Boy doesn't have to grow up because he doesn't have to work for a living. Philip doesn't have to grow up because he doesn't give a damn."

"And what about you?"

"I'm just the lawyer."

Felicity cut off the conversation and let everything go for the moment. "But, Michael, I don't care. I was just making a comment. Our happiness is all I care about."

That, of course wasn't true as a statement of fact but in the context of Michael's determination to see what Philip was up to in Colorado, it was a perfectly coherent statement of his desire.

"When do we head back home?" Felicity asked softly.

"I'll call the airlines, but I'd like to be back home by tomorrow afternoon. I told Theo he could reach me there after tomorrow."

She moved over to him, sat down on his lap, whispered in his ear, tongue brushing the edge of his earlobe, and repeated, "Michael, do you ever doubt that what I want for you is what makes you happy? But before you get your head in Colorado or wherever the hell you're going, I want your body just for now, here with me."

Chapter Two

The most thought-provoking thing in our thought-provoking time is that we are still not thinking - Heidegger

****

Andrew Wolltrip was proud of the wooden, laser-etched nameplate that sat on his desk to inform anyone that might enter his office with whom they were dealing. Sally had given it to him two years ago for Christmas. There beside the nameplate, but facing him, was the silver-framed photo of him, Sally, and the kids, Andrew Jr. and Greta.

Andrew was proud of his position at the BOCC, Board of County Commissioners office for Summit County, Colorado. He had moved to Breckenridge right after he got his BS in Management at Middle Tennessee State. He was the first Wolltrip to graduate from college. He had been here for five years now, and had worked his way up from Assistant Office Administrator to Senior Liaison Officer.

Now he had his own office -- a window office with a view across Main Street's national historical section. The brand new, brick, Summit County government office complex stood in stark contrast to the restored Victorian mining town's US historical site protected architecture.

Sally had decorated the office herself. Andrew vaguely thought the patterned drapes, rattan furniture and butternut breakfront made the place look more like a cathouse than the offices of supreme government but he didn't really have any better ideas.

He looked at his appointment book again for the fifth time this morning. He was having lunch with Barry Hollister at eleven forty five. Meetings with asshole elected commissioners was the worst part of the job. It was already eleven, and before leaving the office he had to meet with some art-type from New York in fifteen minutes.

His intercom rang. Darlene, the matronly, overweight and underpaid secretary squealed, "Mister Theo Boudreaux is here for his appointment." Andrew winced at the sound of her voice. She was assigned to him by seniority. He deserved better. He had read somewhere that Russian employers could advertise a specific look for prospective female employees and even list preferred sexual expertise. The Russians knew how to staff an office.

Andrew looked at his watch. It was 11:03. "Send him on in Ms. Nobel."

No problem. So the son-of-a-bitch was early. It wouldn't take too long to acquaint this outsider with the rules and regulations that should send him on his way, whatever his purposes might be.

The door opened and this uncommonly unpretentious man appeared in the doorway. He was about five foot seven, ruddy-complexioned and dressed in cords with a Nova Scotia plaid flannel shirt. He looked like he could be a native Coloradan.

He had a slight smile that never left his face. Andrew couldn't tell if it was a smile of pleasure, amusement or arrogance. He chose to consider it arrogance. There was no reason to like someone unnecessarily. Theo Boudreaux spoke first in a soft drawl that was obviously not native to Colorado, "Thanks for taking time out of what must be a busy schedule to see me."

Andrew's self-importance took over. "I represent Summit County's Board of Commissioners, and they're always open to -- to input. How can I be of service?"

Andrew hadn't risen. Mr. Boudreaux took the chair that wasn't proffered, but looked welcoming just in front of Andrew's satinwood desk. The rattan squeaked when he sat down. There was the one feature of Sally's furniture that Andrew liked. It was uncomfortable. It kept people from lounging in his presence.

"I represent Philip Alathon. Are you familiar with him?" Mr. Boudreaux asked.

Andrew was not inclined to play guessing games with strangers but Mr. Boudreaux's confident, familiar tone and soft Louisiana accent drew him out against his will. Andrew said, "Philip Alathon? Let's see, do you mean the lieutenant governor's aide?"

"No, I mean Philip Alathon, once referred to as the most exhilarating if not the most destructive force in the contemporary art world. He's living in Wyoming now."

Andrew had two Time/Life art books on his coffee table at home. Sally bought the Dali portfolio to impress Barry Hollister, the newest commissioner, then someone told her that Dali was a phony so she went out a bought the one about Van Gogh. Neither of them impressed Andrew. He was at a complete loss with respect to art-things. Middle Tennessee State had required a humanities course that included art. He had cloudy memories of sleeping through hundreds of slides while a scrawny woman in blue jeans lectured earnestly about form, line, texture and whatever else she could think of to explain what it all really meant. But a picture of a naked woman still looked like a naked woman to Andrew and a picture of a blob of paint was just a blob of paint.

But not wanting to appear uninformed to Mr. Boudreaux, Andrew remembered something from Newsweek, "Did Philip Alathon wrap some building in cellophane?"

Mr. Boudreaux tried to avoid a tone of correction or instruction. "No, that was Christo, but Mr. Alathon and Christo had something in common at one time. Philip would have been mentioned in the same paragraph with Christo ten years ago, in terms of industrial materials or anarchism, or art enterprise. But no, Philip is less well-publicized now. Except for friends and personal communication to a group of followers in San Francisco no one knows much about what he's doing."

Theo paused for a private reflection and thought, "Actually, no one knows what Philip is doing at all." and tried to move the conversation along.

"You ever been to San Francisco?"

Andrew dismissed the question with a shrug. He wasn't going to be further enticed into polite conversation. He enjoyed the sight of Mr. Boudreaux searching for the right diplomatic touch while hunting for a change in the subject. He leaned back in his chair, looked at his watch. It was 11:21. "What was the purpose of our meeting?"

"Well" Mr. Boudreaux replied, "Philip Alathon wants to know what would be involved in getting permission to place a sculpture at the west portal of Eisenhower tunnel. More specifically, what is the connection between the Summit County Commissioners office and the land surrounding the west end of the tunnel?"

Theo passed Andrew a formal description of the property he had obtained at the county clerk's office, and continued: "If someone wanted to do something on that piece of land just to the north of the highway as you come out of the tunnel, what government entities would be involved? From whom would permission need to be gained?"

An opaque curtain fell over Andrew's eyes. A dark cloud circled his brow. How had he let himself be held up like this? How did this guy get in here? Darlene could have taken this question over the phone. The answer is; who gives a shit? Now he had to protect himself from appearing to be ignorant. What should have been a simple office function had become his personal problem. Andrew was taken aback. He had no idea what would be involved. When it came to the land along Interstate 70, all he knew was that Summit County helped with the maintenance in conjunction with the DOT – the Colorado Department of Transportation. The whole idea was ludicrous anyway. Who needed a sculpture by a cellophane artist? And not even a popular cellophane artist at that. A has-been cellophane artist. And how fast can I get this guy out of my office?

He looked at his watch again as if keeping time for the bureaucrat's Olympic competition in removing fools from in front of a desk, "Mr. Boudreaux, your inquiry is interesting. I'll have the appropriate authorities informed and get back to you when I can. I expect it will take them some time to coordinate all that will be involved."

"I couldn't ask for more than your best effort, Mr. Wolltrip," Theo replied. "When should I call you, Tuesday or Wednesday?"

"Oh, you needn't call me. How can I reach you?"

"I'm camping just outside Jackson Hole, Wyoming, a place called Granite. Call us there and leave word with Lem."

Andrew scratched the phone number on Philip Alathon's site proposal and quickly lifted himself from the desk to escort Mr. Boudreaux from the office. The gesture was less courtesy than insurance that he was leaving immediately.

Andrew promised to be in touch as soon as feasible. On his way out to meet with Barry Hollister, he left Philip Alathon's proposal with Darlene. "See what you can find out about this property. Don't spend a lot of time on it."

He was thinking Colorado had enough nuts of its own and didn't need to import one from Wyoming or New York. To do what? Wrap the Eisenhower tunnel? It shouldn't involve a lot of time or effort to officially tell Mr. Exhilarating and Destructive to bug off.

The efficient Darlene sent an immediate electronic inquiry to the title registry data bank in Denver. The response was quick but sketchy. The company that built Eisenhower Tunnel in 1980, Webster Groundworks, Inc., had a lien of some of the property at the west portal. Webster filed for Chapter 11 protection in Kansas City in 1981. Its major creditors were overseas. The holder of the lien now appeared to be HuoYuan Inc. Hong Kong. The law firm that represented HuoYuan was no longer in partnership.

In the blizzard of Colorado bankruptcies in the '80s, one that was settled with little controversy or public disclosure left few traces. With no apparent use for the land except to hold up traffic signs and nothing near the surface on record about it, whatever might be discovered would bring along a complex international paper trail. Andrew had said not to spend a lot of time on it. Darlene had two catchall file drawers: Services to Constituency – Pending, and Services to Constituency - Miscellaneous. 'Pending' meant politically useful and 'miscellaneous' meant who cares? Darlene carefully filed Philip's proposal under miscellaneous and went to lunch.

Along the infinite passages of the Internet which connects electronic databases through a series of local computer hosts, a long dormant intelligent agent had waited ten years for a particular information transfer that would bring it to life and give it purpose. In a host computer in Birmingham, Darlene's query about land at the west portal of Eisenhower tunnel was recognized as an antecedent command. Then an instant later an email message was posted at an address in Seattle, firegarden@geni.com.

■■

After leaving Andrew Wolltrip's office, Theo stopped in the lobby of the county offices and placed a long-distance call to Michael in New York.

Recognizing Theo's voice, Sharon put him right through.

"Michael, Theo Boudreaux here. How was your trip to Acapulco?"

"Great as restful vacations can be. What's this stuff about a sculpture in Colorado? How's Philip? How's Granite?"

"Philip is about the same as always, only blind, and Granite is, believe it or not, not really that much changed from years ago when we were all there together. The biggest change is that just across the river from the campground is an oil well – sort of takes the wilderness aspect away from the scene. As for Philip he's decided his next project would be to build a sculpture -- a monument to the mountain gods -- at the west portal to Eisenhower tunnel."

Michael couldn't suppress a sigh, "What Philip calls a monument could be anything from a raw block of granite to a giant fly swatter that whacked cars as they came out of the tunnel. Whatever, it sounds like he's still got his spirits up."

"I don't think he knows what the design of the piece will eventually be, but we do know that he wants to place it on a piece of land involving county, state and federal bureaucratic oversight.

Even after years of association with Philip, Michael still vaguely believed art had something to do with galleries in the Rue de Seine on the Left Bank, or the Metropolitan Museum, or Mona Lisa. Concern about regulations and government maintenance money seemed out of place in this context..

"And he wants you to donate your outrageous fees."

"Have you talked with anyone yet?"

"Yes, I just met with a guy named Andrew Wolltrip whose title is something like Liaison Officer for the Summit County Board of Commissioners. He said he'd look into the issues--"

"That's unlikely."

"He said he'd look into it and get back to us here in Wyoming."

"That's even more unlikely. If you hear from Wolltrip, give me a call and we'll see what happens next. I'm thinking about coming out there if anything develops."

"Philip thought you might want to join us."

"Right. At the risk of making Philip's intuition right again I'll talk to ya later."

Theo left the county offices in Breckenridge, hitchhiked to the airport, and caught the next plane to Jackson Hole.

It was 9:30 in the offices of the Far Eastern Liaison division of the multinational Chance-Spell/Seattle. The receptionist's first cup of coffee was still hot. She was sleepy. The rhythm of the day hadn't yet set in. The arrival of new e-mail was loudly announced by chirp from her mail client.

Didn't she ask Louis to turn that noise off? The message was flagged urgent and encrypted. Firegarden mail was always coded or sealed and went straight to the desk of Senior Vice-President, Darcy Rios-Doria.

Darcy Rios-Doria was tall, unusually blond with lightly freckled reddish skin and narrow green, slanted eyes. Her coloring reflected the Turkish, Mongolian and Persian heritage of her father's central Asian stock. When she was younger, her striking looks made it difficult for her to be taken seriously with a presentation in a board room or a briefcase in the back of a corporate limo. But she had made her incredibly competent reputation with a willingness to take extraordinary actions that would have been personally destructive had they failed. She acknowledged the power in her looks and took pleasure in knowing that the board, or the commission or the committee was watching her body as well as her presentation. She knew that she could apply her will and intelligence with singular focus and if a male opponent or colleague was thinking with his hormones it would be just that much easier to take him wherever she wanted.

At Chance-Spell, she had oversight of the interests of a diverse group of Hong Kong-based corporations. Some might call her work industrial espionage. Chance-Spell called it Inverse Communication Management. Much of her job was to conceal, with whatever means available, the interests of her Hong Kong group in American businesses and real estate. The reasons for the concealment were not her affair, but she assumed it had political ramifications. She was liberated by the quasi-illegal nature of some of the work and the radical responsibility she took for actions outside of established boundaries. One of her principal clients was HuoYoan.

The work placed her in contact with corrupt or corruptible people. Corruption makes people vulnerable and dangerous. Darcy controlled the best specialists that a Hong Kong front for worldwide nefarious wealth and power could afford but she enjoyed placing herself personally in the field when she was in the mood. She could hack a quota for Russian diamonds out of a computer in Helsinki or bull rush a London barrister into rolling over his client with the sheer force of her intellect (backed up, of course by infinite wealth). But for sharpness of the experience of life, nothing could replace the wire tightness in her abdomen and explosive energy in her chest as she encountered instances of hard physical danger out on the real streets of the world. That intense response to danger always flooded over from her heart into libido.

      She enjoyed the sense of the embarrassment caused when she caught a small county clerk peeking through her loosely unbuttoned blouse at her extraordinary, radiant body while she browsed the files of some meaningless property or company. She could play a skank with nuanced enthusiasm for local hoods, county sheriffs and self-important government inspectors. She cultivated and flaunted her fuck me female persona when it advanced her purposes even as the ruthless Senior Vice President, she visited grief, destruction and humiliation on her rivals at Chance-Spell/Seattle. Darcy Rios-Doria had a job that was truly inclusive and gratifying.

Firegarden was her largest account. She had removed stray references to HuoYuan from the records of a platinum mine in California. She had blocked disclosure of investment in a bankrupt Texas electronics company by bribing a Pennsylvania law firm to represent both the business and the investor. She had sealed a Georgia company's records of an overseas technology transfer by acquiring a high level US Government security clearance.

Darcy Rios-Doria had written the subprogram that was monitoring the property at the west portal of the Eisenhower tunnel in Colorado. The encrypted message in her computer alerted her to the possibility of unpredictable change in a situation that it was her job to ensure remained stable. She had been in Colorado ten years ago and this might be more than a chance to get out into the field which she loved. This was personal and fun.

In camp at Granite, Theo had just returned from the meeting with Andrew Wolltrip. The flight from Denver had just about frayed his nerves to an end. A storm rising in Washington state had been slowly pushing southeast into central Wyoming.

Nonetheless, Theo had survived. He wondered which was worse: the trip, or the brief meeting with Andrew (the self-made-nobody) Wolltrip. But now, here he was at

Granite, safe in the clearing. Without even a "hi, glad you're back, or how'd things go" Philip took up his thoughts as if Theo had never been away and said, "Before we design the sculpture we have to gain access to the site."

Theo wanted to be practical without stepping too much on Phil's delicate new vision a-borning.

"I'm not sure what you have in mind, but what's your guess about the scope of this thing? I mean, how much do you think it'll cost to complete? Some number of millions, I suppose."?

"That's your domain -- probably somewhere in that range."

That was about as practical as Phil was likely to be at this stage. Theo persevered with the pragmatics. "Then you'll need an office. I can help get that started for you. Where? L.A is closer to the money. Or Denver? Or do you want to be even closer to the tunnel?"

"Oh, definitely closer to the tunnel. In fact, I want us to set up a new winter camp just above the tunnel -- on a mountain called 'Coon Hill'." "Jeez. That's near timberline. It'll be colder than shit up there in the winter, and winds, Christ, winds will blow up to 50 miles an hour."

"I know. I'm looking forward to it. But we won't need to spend the entire winter there. Probably out before the first blizzard."

Theo knew that Philip wanted to get a renewed sense of the location -- a feel of the terrain, the surroundings, and the history that drifts around and accumulates in special places. Coon Hill, in addition to whatever it had special of its own, was now made doubly special for being above Eisenhower Tunnel -- a hole through a mountain for the convenience of travelers. Theo also knew that the more difficult an exploration was, the more meaningful -- the more revelatory -- it would be for Philip. Philip would walk right to the edge of an abyss, gaze into it, and dwell around it. Theo just hoped that Philip wouldn't fall in this time.

That night, the first real snow dump of fall was happening all around them. The dump started toward evening, mid-October. Late in the afternoon, precipitation, not much more than frozen mist, appeared in the air. Within a couple of hours, the flakes had become dime-sized, and falling with such density that the view across the valley above the Granite river became nearly opaque – the oil rig was blurred and the top of Gossett Ridge shaded seamlessly into the white of the sky.

"Maybe we should get outta here before we get snowed in" Philip mused. "We have a lotta work to do if we're going to get the sculpture off the ground. How'd it go in Summit?"

"About what you'd expect. This bureaucrat said he'd get back to me as soon as he determined what the process might be. He's a self-important turd whose mind wasn't on our meeting. But I think Michael's going to join us. He'll give us the legal expertise to begin with but we'll still need local contacts."

"Might as well start packing in the morning, and try to be on our way no later than day after tomorrow."

Theo put one more, small log on the fire, moved the coffee pot over the coals, waited until he could hear the fizz of almost-boiling coffee, poured half-a-cup for them both, added a little Southern Comfort, and tried to relax. Eventually, they made their way into the lean-to that had been home since mid-August, and went to sleep.

Chapter Three

"What Philosophy needs is a change of style."

****

Beverly Moore had come to Breckenridge with her boyfriend, Daniel, from Richland, South Carolina where they had met in high school. His family had owned a moderately productive dairy farm, and although he had dutifully tended the Holsteins with his brothers since he could walk, somehow Daniel, the youngest, had grown into the rebellious one. He wanted to be something other than a dairy-farmer. The only problem was, he didn't know what and there weren't a lot of choices in Richland.

He had taken off one winter on a whim, gone skiing at Keystone, Colorado, where he became totally absorbed in the 'ski-bum' way of life. The next fall, he asked Beverly to move to Colorado with him, promising her a better life than she would ever have working in Morton's Apparels in Richland.

She had loved Daniel in high school, allowing him to be her first lover after the Woodsville game their junior year. They had dated off-and-on after high school. The opportunity to move, scary as it had seemed in Richland, just couldn't be passed up, especially after Mo, her dad, had been laid off from the mill.

Frightened, she moved to Summit County with Daniel. The first few days were about getting acclimated, and adjusting to a somewhat different level of being? But, after a few days, she felt she'd arrived. It was indescribably beautiful.

When they moved here, they rented an old Victorian house up on Swede Road, about 1/2 mile from town. But within a little over 4 months, Daniel, unable to find any kind of rewarding work, somewhat a fish out of water and noticeably homesick, moved back home.

Beverly just couldn't move back with him. She had found this great job working at Herr Meinstrom's, making a small hourly rate an hour plus commissions, and her love for the mountains became ingrained. Willie Meinstrom introduced her to skiing, and she had taken to it like a duck to water. She loved the freedom she felt -- schussing down the slopes, knees together, wind blowing her brunette tresses in all directions. It was a sense of freedom she'd never encountered before, in Carolina.

That was how she met Andrew Wolltrip, in the lift-line, Thanksgiving weekend. That holiday, a major tourist attraction for most businesses, she'd worked a half-day, with Willie's blessing. Then she went home by herself. She'd made no plans for a meal, so she stopped by City Market on the way home and got some instant stuffing and a turkey leg. This would be the 1st Thanksgiving that she had spent alone -- or almost alone. After Daniel left, she went to the local animal shelter and got a dog which she named Brownie. Brownie was always there. Brownie was not only her best friend and confidant, but also the only "person" she could talk to. And of course, he was ecstatic to have her home for a day.

It had been snowing most of the day, pretty hard. About 1/2 inch an hour. When she got home, she thought, I'll just have Thanksgiving with Brownie?" She poured herself a glass of wine, started a fire in the fireplace, put her turkey leg in the oven, prepared the stuffing for cooking and called her sister back home, where her mom was having Thanksgiving. Although the family missed her, they seemed preoccupied with their own affairs. After the obligatory pleasantries and wishes for happy holidays, she turned on the Macy's Parade and sat down in the rocking chair in front of the tube.

"I won't be alone next Thanksgiving by God. In fact, I ain't going to remain alone this Thanksgiving." And with that thought, she decided to go skiing for a while, air out the sails so to speak. She ate her Thanksgiving meal quickly, and headed to the slopes.

She had just completed her first run when, in the lift line, some ass-hole skied into her.

"Jeez. Get a grip" she thought as she turned around to see what creep had run across her K-2's. It turned out to be Andrew. After apologies, they made some runs together, and eventually became friends.

Even now she didn't know why she kept seeing him. He was married, stoically dedicated to his government job, and boring. But, there aren't that many reasonably normal people in a ski resort -- mostly ski-bums and real estate agents, scum of the earth -- and as it turned out she didn't have to commit to Andrew.

****

Andrew stood at the door at Meinstroms. He watched Beverly who had just finished dealing with another customer who wanted a 'Ski the Summit' tee shirt and some sunglasses. Beverly glanced up at Andrew, rang up the charge, packed the merchandise in a sack, and flashed her incredible smile to the customer who probably only made the purchase in order to bask in the light of her beauty for a little longer.

Andrew knew that whoever observed Beverly, even for a second, recognized she was beautiful. She was flawless. Perfect peaches and cream complexion, Montana-sky blue eyes, incredible flowing hair. Her figure, unlike Sally's, had remained fortuitously unspoiled by maternity.

Andrew stepped aside to let the customer exit, approached the counter. "Hi Bev, what's happn'g?"

The peaches in Beverly's complexion reddened to strawberry in a fleeting blush. Andrew was flattered beyond wonder by the thought that Beverly could still be moved to blushing in his presence. As much as he was flattered he was psychically aroused.

"A few customers," Beverly said, "scant sales, that's about it. Anything new and exciting on your front?"

The subject of customers and sales didn't contain the warmth that Andrew expected. He thought the blushing was a curiosity.

"No," he said, "just the usual permits and potholes, and some strange guy from Wyoming who wants to construct a sculpture on the west end of Eisenhower Tunnel."

"Really, what kind of sculpture?"

"He spoke of Christo ... ever heard of him."

"Didn't he build a real long canvas wall or something?"

"I don't know about a canvas wall, but I think Christo did wrap some buildings in cellophane. Anyway this fellow represented some other artist, 'Phillip Alathon' he called him. Ever heard of Alathon?"

"No. But I don't keep up with that stuff. A sculpture huh? At Eisenhower Tunnel? Maybe not a bad idea but I think art should be beautiful." Beverly was obviously not in the mood for a chat about art.

Andrew thought he'd check if she was in the mood for another form of creative expression, "You're beautiful. Do we have time for some hanky-panky?

"Not today", and Andrew, maybe not again ... ever."

"Huh?"

Beverly had a look of dread in her eye. She looked like she'd been working up her courage for days. Now the blushing was in context. Andrew thought if he could get her to back off just a little bit her fear would take over and she would give it up for now. Then they could work through whatever reservations she had. He ave Beverly his sternest look but she gave him a level stare back into his eyes "Art, we've known each other for, what, the better part of a year now. You're married. There's no chance for an ongoing relationship with us -- and well, Andrew, I've found this other guy. He's single, available, and pretty good-looking -- not that you're not -- but, anyway, he's available."

"Who is he? What the hell -- why are we doing this? Don't you know how much I love you?" Andrew slapped his hand on the counter top.

Beverly quickly looked up to see if any customers had entered the shop. "Sure I do, Andrew. But you don't love me more than your family ... and I've got to get on with my life."

"So who's the stud?" Andrew asked sarcastically.

"Well, you know him.... it's Barry Hollister, the new County Commissioner

Andrew felt his knees start shaking, and his heart pumping, almost uncontrollably. "Hollister, that son-of-a-bitch. Hadn't even been a commissioner for two weeks before he had the gall to saunter into my office and ask what my job was -- what'd I do here? What the hell does he do here?"

"I thought you liked Barry?" Beverly said.

Andrew was fuming, "How long have you been seeing that twerp?"

"Art don't be cruel. I've always been able to talk to you."

Now Andrew felt himself become fearful and defensive. Beverly was doing her best not to affront his masculinity. She cared about his feelings. She was telling the truth. It was a brilliantly conceived tactic to control the situation.

"I guess he told you he was a famous jock at Yale (Ha!), Cum Laude or something in Business. Rich family with a lot of property in Summit County. Trust fund child. Probably never worked a day in his life."

Art was trying to keep his cool. But he was being betrayed by this nymph from Carolina who worked in a T-shirt shop. Jeez. Nevertheless, she was beautiful and he needed to regain control, "So talk to me about Hollister?" Andrew said through clenched teeth and knew he needed to calm down.

"Well, for starters he's single. And you're not. And you're not about to get divorced. I'm tired of being a mistress, and that's all I'll ever be with you. Ever."

"How long has it been?"

"Just a few weeks. I met him at the Chamber of Commerce mixer. Remember, you asked me to be a volunteer hostess.

"You were supposed to serve him a sausage roll not roll his sausage."

"Art please. This is hard enough. I need to tell you. You asked me to lead him around and make sure he met the key players in the county political arena. You said I was the expert."

"So it's my fault?"

"It's not anybody's fault. He was shy. He had to get up his courage to ask me out. I was charmed. I couldn't help saying yes."

Andrew knew the feeling of being mesmerized by Beverly's beauty. Hollister wouldn't have been the first man in town to bumble his words trying to think of something meaningful to say to her.

Not caring how right she was, and wanting only to keep up his relationship with her, Andrew responded the only way he knew how "You know I love you Bev, and when the timing is right I could leave Sally in a second. But right now, that's just not possible. And you know it."

"Yeh, I know it better than you. Andrew, I know you love me, and I love you as far as I can. But I've my life to live, and there's just no future with you. You know it and I know it. You're a sweet, gentle, kind and fun man. And I'm thankful for and will always remember these times we've had together. But I need a real relationship. It had to happen sometime, and I don't know if Barry is the final answer, but he's a possibility -- the first one I've even considered since meeting you. Come on, gimme a break. If you love me you should want for me what I want. And you shouldn't want to keep me from achieving whatever I want."

"I do love you Bev, and because of that, I can't imagine life without you."

Andrew knew she was serious, "Sure, I want what's best for you. But I also want that to include me."

"I appreciate that Andrew, but that's selfishness on your part. You're a dear, dear man, and you have a lot of virtues, but -- well -- you're taken. And I don't want to interfere with you and your family. Please try to understand."

I'm not going to give you up easily, Bev. Do you understand that?"

Beverly had called him 'sweet, gentle, fun' and finally 'dear.' With a few perfectly timed words she'd transformed him from a lover into a pal. Andrew had to get away before she thought of any other kind words that could shrink his ego to nothing. It was almost 1:30. After Bev thought about it, she would probably change her mind. But for now, he had to get back to the office and the Board of Commissioner's meeting.

"Bev, all I ask is that you give this some more thought; don't make any rash decisions. I'll call you tomorrow."

"OK." Beverly replied and she smiled as Andrew backed out of the door onto the sidewalk.

She would be smiling that devastating smile for Hollister tonight. Smiling and kissing, and he didn't want to think about what else. God he hated that rich bastard. Then he realized that Hollister would be one of the commissioners he would have to wait on this afternoon and thought that there was no end to misery this day.

With his hatred and resentment boiling Andrew walked across Main Street to the Gold Pan Bar. At the curb, he turned back thinking he had seen Barry Hollister's car parked outside. He didn't want to run into Hollister while he was in this mood. Then he thought, "Damn Hollister! I'll kick his ass" and turned again. Before he reached the door he noticed that the car wasn't the same color as Hollister's -- possibly not even the same make.

Andrew entered the Gold Pan. In spite of its tourist-indulgent name, it's on the national historic register. It was a dark neighborhood bar now. It used to be a whorehouse but historical registration doesn't extend its demand for authenticity that far. It still had mismatched tables and chairs. Above a row of un-upholstered barstools, a college basketball game silently played out on television. Andrew's eyes slowly adjusted to the light. He crossed a tiny dance floor and took a seat at the bar. Andrew never drank more than a beer during business hours. Tony brought him one. Tony was a blond athlete with chiseled features of such keen definition that he was almost a caricature of virility. His cheerful arrogance usually annoyed Andrew but Tony knew everything about everybody in town and Andrew was a man who knew enough to cultivate a resource.

"You're lookin' a bit grim and bitter," Tony said, "for a prosperous man living in a mountain paradise.

Andrew drank his beer, "I was planning on something else for my lunch break and got screwed instead."

"You're a county bureaucrat with most of an afternoon left. I'm sure you can find a poor, innocent citizen and take it out on him."

"Do you still have that 24 year old Crown Royal?"

"That's a negative. But I've got some really nice single malt scotches."

"Let me have a double of one of those. I'm drowning my sorrows. It's that or kill some bastard."

"So the citizens are going to have an angry and drunk bureaucrat to deal with this afternoon."

Before Andrew could phrase a reply, Willie Somers and a friend from the water department took seats at the far end of the bar.

Willie nodded a greeting. Andrew scowled a reply.

"What's bothering him?" Willie asked Tony.

"Another mule's been kickin' in his stall."

Willie was prone to be philosophical. "Andrew what do you think is the most common phrase in the English language?"

Andrew snarled, "I don't know."

Willie elaborated, "You know, I mean like, 'The checks in the mail?"

"Yea, or my wife doesn't understand me," Tony suggested.

Willie's friend from the water department proposed, "It wasn't my fault. He told me to do it."

Tony closed the discussion, "There's only one phrase that can be heard anywhere anytime on America -- catch the friggin' ball." Tony turned up the replay of a college basketball game that was playing on ESPN above the bar.

Then a tall, lean, sensational woman in diminutive clothing came from the direction of the restrooms, ducked under the bar and asked Willie and his friend what they wanted.

"That's new?" Andrew asked Tony.

"She came in just a bit ago looking for part-time work. I told her I didn't have anything and, at that exact moment, with her standing right here handing me a letter of recommendation, the phone rang. It was Rachael. She wasn't coming in. She'd come into some money and was going back to Wisconsin. So this new girl took her shift. Just like that. Do you believe in magic?

"That body is magical. What's her name?

"Darcy something."

Darcy Rios-Doria turned into the mirror. Andrew watched her put together a drink for Willie Somers. She was wearing makeup that strangely accentuated the lines around her eyes and mouth. It made her look older or just more thoroughly worn. Her hair was dyed a bright, almost metallic, red. Her tight black skirt was high. Her sheer white bodice was low and she wouldn't have looked more at home tending bar if the word 'barmaid' had been tattooed on her bosom.

Darcy swayed her hips and stirred. She blessed Willie Somers with an open, guileless smile. With the white edge of her blouse barely clinging to visible breasts blooming in a field of delicate freckles, she leaned toward Willie and offered him a drink. She asked softly, with just a hint of deference to his superior wisdom and judgment, "Will this do?" Willie's eyes were shining. Andrew thought he could actually see his tongue hanging out. This woman could have passed Willie a plague rat in a glass of arsenic and asked, "Will this do?" and he would have drunk with relish and been sorry that he died before he could leave a big tip.

Andrew's eyes swept down the long curves of Darcy's body and over to Tony, "I'll bet that body knows some stories."

"It would probably keep you up all night talking."

Sara Muslik and Brenda Davis took seats at the bar next to Andrew. He knew them from the ski slopes. They were instructors. It was beginning to creep into Andrew's consciousness that young women of their age might regard him as an older man but he fought the idea. Darcy approached to serve them. All of the palpable eroticism that had liquefied Willie Somers was put away in an instant. To Sara and

Brenda, Darcy was just another girl doing a job. They wanted beer.

The basketball game on TV came to the half. Sara made a comment about a basketball player she had dated in college. The announcer said, "With the new hand check rule, the Bobcats are getting good dribbles."

Darcy returned with the beer. She said, "Dribbling is about all I've been getting recently. I'm looking for some fire hose action if you know what I mean, and you can keep the hand checking." Sara giggled and Brenda nodded enthusiastically. The women understood one another completely.

Sara added, "My college boyfriend said he could show me how to drive the lane."

"Take it strong to the hole." Brenda squealed blushing. "Always dribble before you shoot."

Andrew felt like he was eavesdropping on some intimate feminine business. The women he knew didn't talk like this in front of men. These three were acting like he wasn't there. He looked up from his drink straight into the scalding green eyes of Darcy Rios-Doria. She held his gaze just long enough to tell him that she knew he was watching her and listening. Then she turned away.

****

When Andrew returned to work, Darlene had a call from Seattle that had been holding for ten minutes. He took it in his office. "This is Andrew Wolltrip." A distracted woman's voice said, "Just a moment please," then a richer, more authoritative woman's voice came on the line. "Thanks for taking my call Mr. Wolltrip. I represent The Stollen Gallery in Washington. We have some interest in original photographic documentation of work by an artist named Phillip Alathon. I understand that I might be able to reach him through you."

Andrew wondered how he'd become this ridiculous artist's appointment secretary. "I have a phone number in Wyoming," Andrew said sharply, "I'll give you back to my secretary."

The voice said, "Thank you" and Andrew buzzed Darlene. Then he wondered what the woman's name was and how she had known to use him to reach someone he'd met just two hours ago. He returned to the outer office to ask Darlene, "Who was that?"

"I don't know," she said, "I thought you knew her."

At The Gold Pan Bar, Darcy Rios-Doria hung up the phone and put a Wyoming phone number in her wallet.

Chapter Four

"Making itself intelligible is suicide for philosophy." Heidegger

****

The day after he returned to Granite, Theo began preparations for the move to Summit County. Amazing how stuff accumulates.

They had driven a rented van in with only a few items. Now, there were heavy pots, pans, lanterns, axes, shovels, provisions and, of course, the requisite books. During their stay, they had made the campsite amazingly livable. There were tables made with short pine limbs tied together between trees with binder's twine. The lean-to they had constructed from canvas supported by available small-tree trunks became the storeroom and it was loaded with gear.

After a year of blindness, Philip had become surprisingly adroit at working with things using only his sense of feel. When he could see, his art always was about bringing the mute world of conventional values to hand and tearing them apart to reveal meaning. But blindness had made him more contemplative or at least had circumscribed his actions.

Philip said, "The truth has to come from someplace other than the artist's dreams." And after a pause, "Blindness tempts one to dream doesn't it?"

"I don't know," Theo replied. "I don't remember any dreams. I think I do all my dreaming on purpose when I'm awake."

"Blindness darkens the soul and prepares it for visions of heaven."

"And heaven is just a dream."

"If it's not backed up with a plan for action."

Theo didn't believe Philip was worried about getting to heaven. "You mean a plan to get to heaven? There are a lot of those available--blueprints and specifications for all manner of pathways, ladders, and secret doors that are designed to vanish the moment that they're completed. So no one knows what was successful and what wasn't."

Philip wasn't talking about life after death. "That's not what I'm talking about. I've enjoyed my work as an anarchist. In the microcosmic world of art I was a destroyer, a prankster and a cynic who opposed everything. But underneath the hostility must have been a profound optimism. I must have believed that the truth was just under the surface of lies and conventions and would shine forth as soon as I cleared away all the historical rubble."

Theo repeated, "A shining mountain under the rubble."

"In my life I've cleared away a lot of stuff--and underneath?--there's just more stuff."

Philip picked up a stone. He could classify the textural surface of a stone or leaf with what was apparently a photographic tactile memory. He said, "Can a rock lie. Can it be false? As soon as I pick it up it becomes something other than a rock. In my hand it's what I make of it -- and I can make it into a lie."

Theo said, "Maybe as an affirmation of life--"

"Life needs affirming only to a pessimist."

"--a lie is worth more than the truth."

"That sounds like the opinion of a poet. Inventing lies is your work isn't it?"

"I was thinking more in terms of inventing heaven. You brought it up."

Taking advantage of unseasonably warm days, Philip had set out to know, by feel, the appearance of the rocky bottom of Granite Creek. He said, "The experience of moving of water against the immobile stone is a sensory extreme that borders on pain."

Theo said, "O little world what rapturous star will be born today."

Breaking camp was a challenge. The only way to get out would be by snowmobiles and snowshoes. They had been sleeping under the stars. Now they were stretching a tarpaulin out away from the lean-to for shelter. So while Philip mused over the nature of the sculpture, Theo prepared pallet-like sleds for packing gear out. They would tie them behind the snowmobile and pull them down to the Granite Gap lodge, where Lem Hodgins would allow them to store all the gear in the back shed for a few days, until they moved it on.

Lem seemed ok. He had grown up at the lodge here along the Hoback and when his Dad died, he just assumed control. His mother had moved to Colorado. His brother and sister couldn't have cared less. To be honest, Lem didn't even know where his brother was. Lem had never married, and lived a fairly reclusive life, just running the lodge, hunting, fishing, and surviving.

Philip and Theo had bought most of their provisions from Lem for the past three months and infrequently, he brought messages to them. Lem loved an excuse to get away from the lodge for a legitimate reason. He'd put the "closed" sign on the front door, get in his jeep, and drive the 6 miles up the washboard, gravel road to where Philip and Theo were camping. He commented that they were staying up Granite Creek more than the typical camper and once asked what kind of business they were trying to conduct from there but didn't pay much attention when they tried to tell him. He knew only that Philip was a recovering, blind artist.

Theo looked forward to Lem's trips up to their campsite. He always had some great stories -- about huge elk, brown bears, his Mom in the Granite River panning for gold, and his brother Les, driving cattle across the Green River in early spring. Lem was a good storyteller, sometimes closing his eyes and allowing his words to verbalize scenes from his imagination in amazingly lucid detail. Theo admired the intellectual innocence of Lem. One thing about "real" mountain people, the pioneer spirit was in their souls -- nothing couldn't be overcome -- and "cost-benefit ratios" had to do with the cost of a satisfied, well-lived human life, not dollars.

Theo asked Lem if he had any storage facilities they could rent for a short term, and Lem told Theo the shed behind the lodge could be used. The shed was mostly empty anyway.

For three days, Theo trekked stuff down to Granite Gap in the rented snowmobile, stored it in Lem's shed, and prepared to get on down to Summit County, Colorado.

On the fourth day as Theo brought the last load up to the shed he noticed the door open and all of their gear inside bundled and tied. He crossed to the back of the lodge, crunching across snow that had thawed a bit in yesterday's sunshine and refrozen last night. He called out to Lem. There was an emphatic pause then the door hinge squeaked as Lem came out onto the porch. "It got colder last night," Lem said. The coffee cup in his hand was steaming in the brisk morning air. He was glaring into the steam as if waiting for a sign to begin something important.

Theo said, "I've got the last load. Did you want me to organize our gear in the shed?"

"No. I want you to take it all out." Lem said, "I changed my mind. I want to do something with that shed this week. Maybe I'll tear it down. I'm tired of looking at it."

Theo knew mountain people could make up their minds using criteria that were not always obvious to lowlanders but Lem was being harsh. He must know how disruptive this change of mind would be.

"Can we leave it here till we make other arrangements?"

"No it needs to get out."

"We brought it here so we could move it all at one time. Do you need more money for storage?" Theo knew it was a mistake to try to influence Lem with money but he was trying to think of something

"This ain't a mini-warehouse. And quit asking questions. You're not gonna argue me down about this."

This was strange behavior, even for Lem--why was he angry?

Theo said, "I'm not arguing. I'm just asking."

"If you want the answer, and it ain't gonna do you any good to know it, you can't rent the shed or anything else from me because I might not be here when you get back."

Theo said, "Where you going?"

"I want you and Philip to get away from me. He's caused me enough trouble already.

"Then, I'll have to go down and get the van today."

"Right now."

"I can be back in three or four hours." Now Theo was angry. "You can wait that long to tear the shed down?"

Lem returned to the lodge.

There wasn't any way that Theo could avoid respecting Lem's wishes about that. He didn't want to press Lem into doing something drastic to force the issue. He certainly, didn't want to replace all of this gear. It had taken months to accumulate and he had every piece of it just the way he wanted it.

Theo parked the snowmobile out of the drive and set out to hitchhike to Jackson Hole. On the way he wondered what Philip had done to anger Lem. Then he thought, Lem wasn't angry. He was afraid. Theo wanted to hurry but a hitchhiker can't actually put more urgency in his thumb. A man out on an open road who looks like he needs something -- urgently -- won't get a ride.

When Theo returned in the van, four hours later, the lodge was closed and the snowmobile was gone. New snow was falling and there were no tracks out of the area.

Theo was fuming. Lem's annoying pigheadedness had turned into obstructive larceny. He wanted to find Lem and do something melodramatic to force an explanation out of him. He called Lem loudly. Then he called loudly and angrily. The Hobacks echoed his frustration. He tramped up and down in the snow in back of the lodge but there was nothing of substance to strangle, dismember or maim so he gave it up and resigned himself to hiking up to Granite.

He was too tired to be angry when he arrived at the campsite but Lem's hostility and fear had been directed against Philip, and Theo had enough energy left over to be worried. He would be comforted to know that Philip was safe and that they were on their way out of Granite for a while. Then he saw the snowmobile parked behind the lean-to.

Snow was continuing to fall. The contours of the snowmobile were disappearing under a steady accumulation. There was no sign of P. Theo called to him and there was no answer. The fire had died down. He kicked through a shallow drift to the front of the lean-to. Philip was not inside. A bloody knife blade stained the canvas at the edge of the entrance. Under the new snow, the campsite looked like it had been deserted for days. Theo called again.

Philip's voice nearby said, "Why are you shouting?" Philip was sitting on a log near a cedar bush a few feet away. He was wrapped in a blanket and his head and shoulders were covered with snow. He had been shut up in his own thoughts and indifferent to the snowfall. Now he blended in perfectly with the bush. Theo turned back the flap of the lean-to expecting to see the bloody knife. Instead he saw the red edge of a Powerbar wrapper amplified by his anxiety into a vicious instrument of pain and death.

Theo said, "You scared the shit out of me. I hope your fuckin' toes are frozen off." He was getting the fire going again. "Didn't you wonder where I was or what was going on around the camp here with insane hunting lodge proprietors crashing through on stolen snowmobiles and that kind of thing?"

Philip said, "I heard you drive up several hours ago but I assumed you were working on something."

Philip's mind worked that way. He could think that someone might be so intent on what he was doing that he'd be passing back and forth, nearby for several hours and forget to say hello.

The fire was hot and Philip moved closer to it. He did feel the cold. He just chose to ignore it some time. A little coffee and Comfort would warm him up. When Theo brought the coffee pot from the lean-to there was a scrawled note from Lem attached to it: WORMWOOD.

Chapter Five

"There are no facts, only interpretations" - Nietzsche

****

With Philip in the passenger's bucket seat and a month's accumulation of gear stuffed in the back, Theo turned the rented van toward Bondurant. In a couple of hours, they would be along where the great Green River cuts its path across the plains. They would probably be in Rock Springs for lunch. There wasn't much change of scenery for Theo to describe -- mountains way off to the right, barren plains off to the left between the road and the Green River.

In the absence of scenic descriptions from Theo, Philip intermittently thought aloud. "Do you ever wonder how our lives would have gone if we hadn't bumbled into those philosophy classes at Tulane?"

"Sounds like the plot of a bad art movie." Theo answered without taking his eyes off the narrow road. "First the characters take a philosophy course and end up driving to Colorado talking about Kant's Schematism. Then, in the second part, they don't take a philosophy course and drive around talking about women, sex and football. What would we think without having been exposed to academic philosophy?"

Philip stuck to philosophy. "Heidegger's discussions of Kant's Schematism turned me down the road to art. Knowledge amounts to what Kant called 'free play' between the imagination and the understanding. I thought this might be the theme of a dissertation, but not in an academic dialogue. For me, the imaginative part of knowledge had to be metaphor."

"Metaphor is the world-constituting power of the existential human. It's the point in experience where history and consciousness enter into the truth. Knowledge can't be understood without understanding metaphor. So to discuss Heidegger's (and Kant's) understanding of understanding, I was going to talk about metaphor. And I was going to do it imaginatively, creatively, that is, metaphorically. In order to discuss metaphor, I had to use it. Unfortunately, The Kantian, Dr. Greene, and the Aesthetician, Mrs. Fowler, didn't think that was proper academics. That just exemplifies what's wrong with academic philosophy."

Theo rejoined as a logician and programmer. "They might be right.

If you were talking about mixing the expert discourse of enlightened philosophers with the irrational, self-authenticating intuition of poets and prophets you could be turning your back on a lot of what we, for lack of a better word, call academic civilization."

"That's right. They wanted a civilized, sterile treatise destined for a library of congress number, ten copies, and no readership. Young Dr. Milner was more liberal. Like all liberals he was open minded and generous as long as his own18th Century rationalist methods weren't really threatened. He seemed willing to listen to me, but in his desire to acquire tenure, he was afraid to champion anything really controversial. He couldn't see why I wouldn't temporarily stuff my ideas into a traditional, doctoral dissertation format and get on with my career. Only Dr. Kamburg, 19th Century German specialist seemed willing to listen."

"He was an unreconstructed romantic." Theo remembered.

"He was a romantic and still in his heart believed that Philosophy was about God, freedom and immortality and not a good living on a tenured salary."

"That's because he had tenure himself. He could vicariously exult in your sturm and drang as long as it was your ass that got hung out to dry."

"He was old and ridiculed by the rest of the faculty anyway, if that's what you mean. But in fact his classes exemplified my understanding of the nature and spirit of philosophy."

"Old and ridiculed?"

"We met at his house every Wednesday night. For three hours, we would discuss this or that topic, and it wasn't the topic that was important. It was the caliber of the discussion -- the entry of nuances, taking tangential roads beyond mere logical contradiction all the way to absurdity. Time was discussed with reference to the field hand's hearing the church bell toll, signaling day's end. Space was the distance between lovers. When someone wanted to define art, Kamburg would hold up both hands, palms outward, wanting silence then remind us that what we were doing right then could qualify as art if it were excellent. And we would talk a little more, and be challenged to take heart, as my Dad had challenged me so many years before, to "do it right or not at all", to do what was important, excellently. Philosophy had forgotten what kind of art it was. It took itself too seriously and its sterility demanded a change of style. Heidegger first articulated this possibility for me in <u>Poetry, Language and Thought</u>. "

Theo persisted. "If philosophy abandons its narrow rationality for the boundlessness of literature then it's just another interesting story. It gives up its unction as a place to test ideas and prepare them for insertion back into the general culture."

Philip pausing for a second to reflect on Theo's interruption, "After 'class'. Kamburg always poured each of us, there would only be 5-6 signing up for his course, a glass of California wine from a half-gallon jug, and we would take our ideas out into the general culture of the Napoleon House on Chartres for some Guinness Stout and a muffaletta. At Napoleon House, forgetting the real lesson of Kamburg, as if driven by some unknown demon of the ordinary, my classmates would resume their pedagogical bullshit and try to intellectualize the class to fit the lesson into this- or that- pigeonhole. I was usually savoring the fare, and always enjoying my quiet interpretation of the table conversation. It was as if I had created the scene for my own illumination, sort of creating déjà vu. Those conversations were more real and familiar than anything I had ever known. As each moment came into focus, it was distinctly new to me but just as clearly some place and time where I had always been and always would be. They were instances of deja vu that I was creating."

"I couldn't keep telling all of them that to talk about metaphor, you had to use it. The majority wouldn't work with me on those terms anyway. I couldn't just write a metaphor about metaphor. I had to show that creativity was creating Deja vu. I had to find room to improvise. I became a fine arts student and ultimately a fine artist.

But Nietzsche had been the point of departure for Heidegger and I've never put all of that aside. A sentence in the first chapter of Zarathustra remains indelible in my psyche: 'One still must have chaos in one's life to give birth to a dancing star.' That's what I'm making as a gift to these mountains 'Dancing Star'."

Theo sighed. "I'm pleased to find out that you have something definite in mind. I was beginning to wonder."

"I'm pulling a lifetime's worth of influences together into a created deja vu. It will be the newest and oldest of my experiences. The ultimate form will resemble Cheri."

"Would you say that again? I'm sure I misunderstood you."

"I don't think so. Cheri's the ballet dancer I've lusted after forever. Cheri, who studied at L'Academie in Colorado, under Felice Peres and later became a member of the Houston ballet. At age 37 she was the most beautiful, nubile, well-formed, sensuous woman I've ever known. We had four days of sheer lust together in Jackson Hole. To the music of Keith Jarrett's 'Koln Concert', she danced around the living room, wearing only a lace bra and panties, with an abandon I knew I would one day have to reproduce. She's become the personification of Dancing Star."

"What do you tell students who want to make a sculptures of their girlfriends."

"I'd tell them they'll get an F for being full of shit."

"Well?"

"I'd tell them they have to wait to make sculptures of their girlfriends until they have the creative power to get it right. Now is the time for me. Dancing Star will be beautiful and significant.

"So we're talking about sex after all."

"You know that G. W. Hardy in "A Mathematician's Apology" spent over a hundred pages trying to explain what made a pure mathematical formula 'significant'. In the end, for Hardy, what gave significance to a mathematical formula were specific aesthetic qualities -- non-triviality, unexpectedness, inevitability and economy -- simply stated "purity". From a broader perspective a significant piece had to have generality -- an ability to connect many different ideas - - its metaphorical capacity -- its beauty.

They were about 12 miles from Rock Springs. Theo was hungry. Since awaking this morning he had trekked the final load of gear down from Granite to I 5, hitchhiked to Jackson Hole to pick up the rented Van, driven back to Granite Gap, and loaded all the stored gear.

"You hungry?" Theo asked.

"Huh. Oh yeah, sure. What time is it? Where are we?"

"Almost to Rock Springs

At the Board of Commissioners meeting, Andrew took his usual seat with his back to the window and set up to take the minutes of the meeting. This was usually a good opportunity to watch the commissioners as they entered the meeting room. Andrew thought he could tell a lot about their alliances and rivalries by their posture, jokes and positioning as they made their way around to the seats. But today all he wanted to know was where Barry Hollister was. If he was at the meeting he couldn't be making out with Beverly.

Andrew was thinking that Hollister might not show up at all. The son of a bitch didn't have to work. He'd been fishing in Montana for six days. A playboy like Hollister probably wouldn't think this little meeting was worth coming back for. Nothing's important if you don't have to earn it. The privileged shit.

Barry Hollister was the last into the room. Andrew lowered his eyes to the minutes as the chairman of the board, Lawrence Richgood, called the meeting to order and introduced Barry as the new commissioner. "How was the fishing in Montana, Mr. Hollister?"

Hollister was drawn into the center of attention. Everybody is always sucking up to the bastard, Andrew thought. Now he was giving his first report to the county commissioners on a fishing trip.

"As many of you know," Hollister began, "the Madison River, offers some of the finest blue-ribbon water in all the world. There are cutthroats in the Yellowstone, giant rainbows over at Henry's Fork in Idaho, and of course, in the great Madison. I met with a lot of luck on the Madison, especially that stretch just below Quake Lake northwest of West Yellowstone. Caught 8-10 rainbows over 17 inches, on Caddis and Grasshoppers. And no place in the West makes bigger or better hamburgers than the Grizzly Bar overlooking the Madison. At almost any hour after, say 3 p.m., you can go there for food, drinks, camaraderie with other Class A fishermen whose tales have the kind of credibility which only obtains from being humbled by years of contest for THE CATCH. Thanks for asking."

Amid a smattering of amused applause, Hollister took his seat.

In the same moment, Lawrence Richgood asked for reports from each of the department heads.

In more or less alphabetical order, each of the heads of committees delivered reports on their particular area of interest. There would be reports from the Ambulance, Animal Control, Tax Assessor, Buildings & Grounds, Clerk & Recorder, Communications, Community Development, Environmental Health, Coroner, Data Processing, District Attorney, Extension Services, Finance, Library, County Manager, Road and Bridge, Sheriff, Social Services, and Treasury departments. Topics ranged from mosquito control to child support to Wet Child Conferences to septic system regulations. The Road and Bridge functionary, James Bagnold began with a report on how well some 1/4 million dollars had been spent on road improvements on Ute Pass, Swan Mountain Road, Sweeney Road, and County Road 579. There were other improvements on Five Mile Vista and the Royal highway.

Andrew thought that a know-nothing and do-nothing like Hollister would probably consider this all oh so booooorrrrinnnggg but Andrew understood that this was the substance of politics in a democratic bureaucracy. Over a period of three hours each department head would proselytize about a glowing accomplishment and detail how much more could be done with better support on the budget. The intent was to rationalize, justify or celebrate the expenditure of public funds. The coordination of these reports and the allocation of resources so that the funds could actually be acquired and spent was Andrew's job. Without his practical work all of the big ideas were meaningless and all of the planners and schemers were impotent – at least that was how he felt.

Hollister sat silent through the whole meeting, but when Lawrence Richgood asked if there was any new business, he raised his hand.

"Mr. Hollister. Again, welcome aboard. What's your question?"

"Please call me Barry, and may I call you Lawrence?"

"Of course."

"Well, I know I'm new to this position, and perhaps my question is out of line, but, don't we have any Arts Committees?"

Andrew thought it would take a naive dilettante like Hollister to bring up something as far reaching as an Art Committee at this point in the meeting with everyone already shuffling in their chairs and leaning towards the door. Andrew's eyes were riveted to Hollister with gleeful expectation that he was about to make a fool of himself.

"I understand the importance of septic system regulation," Hollister began, "but I wanted to expand a bit on some larger ideas."

In five seconds Hollister had already screwed a relationship with one commissioner by suggesting the smallness in his department's ideas. This was going to be great.

Hollister continued, "The solitude of fishing really brings things together in my mind. I mean, we represent communities that are transforming themselves into a world-class resort area. While I can appreciate and respect the fine job done by each of the extant departments, I can't help but wonder if we couldn't use a little creative marketing.

The visitors we want to invite to our county are mostly wealthy, sophisticated, and worldly people. They take the maintenance services we provide for granted. If our economic base is tourism, we could improve by putting some part of our energies into reating a climate, which the tourist will recognize as unique? Something which will make him go back and say 'have you ever seen' or 'have you ever been to'.... Shouldn't we do something to make this county unique?

Are we just another ski complex, or are we going to lead the way into the 21st century? Becoming more visionary will directly benefit our economy and forge a community identity. I know from my campaigning that my constituents are open to this. A number of them voiced the need for a more unified marketing approach and vision for the whole county. We have a film festival, but is it recognized anywhere else? Couldn't ... shouldn't we aspire to Telluride or even Cannes? We have music festivals, but the emphasis is on bluegrass rather than something international and challenging like modern classical or jazz. Our cultural events are local and mediocre. Instead, shouldn't we position ourselves on the leading edge of all that we do? I don't think we need to be controversial but I do think we could be engaged."

Hollister sat down, apparently embarrassed and out of breath but expecting a practical response from the commission to his emotional diatribe. The other commissioners appeared to have listened to him, but it was uncertain whether they heard.

"Your points are well taken, Barry." Lawrence offered after a moment.

Andrew was out of order but he couldn't help interjecting loudly, "I would propose that we make Mr. Hollister our special envoy to the Cannes Film Festival."

The Coroner amplified the sarcasm in Andrew's proposal, "That's a good idea, Andrew." He said, "When those French dudes want to move their operation to Colorado we'll be ready for them."

The County Manager was more supportive, "I don't think we can recreate Cannes topless beaches but we might use some more art up here. Don't you think?

Lawrence cut off the jokes, "Thanks. Barry, we'll put your ideas in the perspective of our budget constraints as time goes by. Is there any more new business?"

After a brief silence, Lawrence adjourned the meeting and mentioned that there would be refreshments in the anteroom for anyone who wanted them.

Andrew went into the "anteroom" which was basically the bar, and ordered a Perrier. Three or four of the commissioners were introducing to themselves to Barry Hollister and awkwardly trying to make up for what could have been a disrespectful rejection of his views. After they had replaced disrespect with patronizing curiosity they moved over to the fireplace nd took up heated discussions of ski conditions and weather reports.

Barry Hollister was alone at the bar. Andrew ordered a scotch and steeled himself for a line of approach. He wanted to let Hollister know who was in charge. "Mr. Hollister, I'm Andrew Wolltrip, Senior Liaison Officer for BOCC. Congratulations on your election, and, by the way, I listened to your talk. It was all a bit -- how can I put this? – premature mostly because of budget restraints. I don't think it's going to work now or at any time in the future to tell you the truth but I put it down in the minutes and it'll be there for anyone who wants to see what you want to contribute to the county. If there's anything else I can do to help let me know."

There was a lot more hostility in Andrew's voice than he wanted.

Hollister looked confused and said, "Thanks."

Andrew said, "Sure." And turned away.

"Beverly, mentioned you." Hollister said with a lot of hesitation.

Andrew turned around. God this guy has no sense of timing at all, thought Andrew. "Yes," he said We've been friends a while. She told me she'd seen you a couple of times."

"That's right. Nice girl and an astonishing beauty out here among the mountain Amazons. I really think a lot of her. I just thought I should say something."

Andrew suppressed a sigh. "A lot of men in Breckenridge speak highly of her beauty and other talents. I'm glad we had a chance to talk."

Andrew's course was clear. As he finished his drink and headed back to the office he thought, "I'm going to flatten that prick."

On Saturday mornings Beverly liked to sleep late if Brownie would let her and spend the rest of the morning working around the house. She was just pouring her first cup of coffee when the phone rang. It was Andrew.

"Good morning Bev. It's time to get out of bed and enjoy this beautiful day." He was trying to be extra cheerful but there was an edge to his voice.

"How are you Andrew?" Beverly asked as casually as she could muster. She was praying that he was getting over their affair.

"Are you awake?" Andrew said pointedly. "Are you alone?" and Beverly knew he was still thinking about her.

Beverly took a deep breath. "I'm alone Andrew but I can't talk right now."

"No, listen. I wanted to pass along some information. I got a call from Mary Donahue yesterday or was it the day before." Beverly could tell that Andrew was trying not to sound like he was looking for any excuse to call. "You've met Mary. You've seen her around the county commission's offices. She's a pseudo-patron of local arts and crafts."

"I know Mary Donahue quite well. Her daughter works at the shop at Christmas."

"Then maybe you know that five or six years ago there was some discussion about the formal establishment of a quasi-governmental arts body. Mary Donahue was one of the advocates. Back then, the discussions were mostly in about the ULLR fest and judging snow/ice sculpting."

"I had forgotten that.

"That's why I called. She's heard about your friend Barry's diatribe to the commissioners and wants to speak with him. She's an old community activist who still reads the minutes of government meetings in the Gazette. I wanted to call you today because I forgot yesterday and maybe you would want to try to get her in touch with Hollister right away."

Beverly was touched by Andrew's generosity. "That's really nice of you." She said.

"I'm just trying to be helpful." Andrew replied. "What did you expect?"

"I thought you'd be mad at me and resentful of Barry."

"I'm not mad Beverly. I'm hurt and disappointed. I love you and I'll never forget that."

"I miss you too." Beverly had tears in her eyes. "Maybe we can get together sometime soon."

"Real soon." Andrew said. "And don't forget to call Mary."

"Oh No. I'll call today."

****

Beverly picked Barry up in the early afternoon and they drove to Mary Donahue's house. Beverly had planned to show Barry some of Brownie's favorite hiking rails but Andrew's call had made her excited to work together with Barry on something that was important to both of them. She had never been to Mary's house and was following directions up toward Tarnshore drive south of town. Barry couldn't help but become enthralled with the scenery. The River Road south out of town is one of the most spectacular drives in all of Colorado.

Barry's mind meandered from the mountains to the river. "The river itself," he said, "has unfortunately become mostly barren of decent trout south of town. It looks great ... looks like there ought to be tons of brookies waiting to become dinner for someone ... but they just aren't there, probably because the river itself comes and goes, sometimes above ground, sometimes below. The fish must be confused, and in defense of their own sanity, abandoned this part of the river."

Nevertheless, it was a beautiful drive out to Tarnshore.

Mary's instructions had been to the point and accurate. They turned left, stayed to the right, and the house was the third one on the right. As they pulled into the driveway, Beverly and Barry took a moment to admire the house. It was huge, at least 4,000 square feet, tri-level, gunmetal gray, with lots of balconies. It had a welcoming ambiance that drew them out of the Toyota and up onto the front porch.

As they walked up the steps, Mary's face emerged translucent in the leaded glass of the front door and welcomed them in. "Beverly it's nice to see you. Have you really never been to visit me? And I'm sure you're Barry Hollister" as she kissed Beverly on the cheek and extended her hand to Barry.

"And you must be the Mary Dohahue I've heard so much about. Pleased to make your acquaintance. Wow, what a place you have here."

"Thanks. I don't need this much room or responsibility but I enjoy it.

They walked through the oak entryway, into a monstrously inviting den that combined a lived-in feeling with a casual balance of colors and textures that revealed an ingrained and probably inherited good taste. The wall hangings were oriental and probably original. The furniture was expensive but comfortable.

"I've been working in my greenhouse all morning, finalizing preparations for the advent of winter." Mary said. "We only have a couple more weeks. I'm surprised you caught me near a phone. I'm still not used to having a telephone in my apron pocket. When it rang I almost dropped the Impatiens plant I was holding."

"I'm sorry." Beverly said.

"No. I'm glad you called. It's been weeks since I've had a visitor. My daughter's friends are in and out of here all the time. In fact I'm not sure that there aren't a couple of them living here now. But I'm glad to have company of my own. I need a reason to fix my hair and put on the kettle for an afternoon tea. Can I offer you some?"

Beverly and Barry accepted the offered seats and said, "Thanks," for the tea.

Mary brushed back her salt-and-pepper hair and poured. "I read about your -- your BOCC indoctrination," she said to Barry, "and thought you might be in need of a supportive voice after what must have been an anxious commencement. You're somewhat of a neophyte here, and you must feel it. So I called Mr. Wolltrip. I understand you know him Beverly."

The small town gossip network was working perfectly. Beverly flushed hotly and hid her face behind a teacup. Barry was too engrossed in Mary's story to notice.

Many continued, "I don't want to be patronizing, rather I want to just give you the benefit of my experience here. Several years ago, I along with Mary Burton, Sally Engstrom, Stephanie Lundberg and a few others, all of whom have left Summit County now, tried to initiate some support and funding for a quasi-governmental committee whose role was to basically do no more than acknowledge the relevance of artsy stuff in Summit County. We had questionable success ... but we at least felt good about our attempt. Then, the county as we know it now, was in its infancy. Ridge and French Streets were still gravel, and there were no "malls" on Main Street. Is this boring to you?"

"Not at all. Go ahead."

"I can best inform you by letting you in on some recent history directly related to what you're about to attempt. Five or six years ago, a pretty good artist, Remosche was his name, wanted to place a piece of abstract, stained glass sculpture down in Quadrangle Park in Frisco. Not knowing what to do or how to address the situation, the town council, after consulting with the local arts council, decided to mail ballots to all local box holders in town. I can't recall exactly, but of the 2,000 or so ballots mailed, about 150 were returned -- in some circles a representative sample, in others, not."

"Of the 150 or so returned, about 50% approved of the sculpture and its concomitant cost to the taxpayers. Seems like the piece was called 'Wind of the Mountains' or something like that. Anyway, the major objection of the seventy-five or so who objected was the expense. Even though half of the cost had to e raised by private sources in order for the project to proceed, the remaining $4-5,000 would become additional taxes -- to the tune of about $1.50 per year per taxpayer.

"There was spirited debate in the town council meetings for a few sessions. Sally Engstrom's husband was a councilman then, and he was so vehement in his opposition to the project that they almost divorced. The mayor, I forget her name now, made an issue about the interpretation of the results of a rather 'unscientific ballot' and questioned, basically, the public's intelligence in reading and understanding the issue of the ballot. At some point, a statuette of the proposed piece got placed in front of the post office for everyone to view. But finally, the towns advertising advisory committee, headed by the antiquated views of Cross, David and McCross, interjected that the piece was not consistent with what they perceived to be the town's image."

"Of course this brought about more discussion about just what the town's image 'ought' to be. The image issue had been addressed only obliquely in the original ballot. Some respondents wanted representational art -- whatever that is -- others wanted no public art at all, while still others felt that 'Wind of the Mountains' would positively enhance the town image."

"Believe it or not, in the end, the town council voted to grant an easement for the placement of the sculpture. This would have seemed a major coup for the arts council, but the process took so long that

Remosche lost heart and headed for Montana or somewhere else, to do his thing."

Barry was inhaling all this like a junkie.

"Mary, Sally and Stephanie have since moved away and I'm the only one left of the original arts crew. My husband took off for San Francisco and left me with his bank account and this house. For the past several years I've more or less just hung out here, tending my plants and -- and not doing much else. I've a bent for activism concerning the arts, but there really hasn't been anything to get active about recently. Then I heard of your spiel at the last commissioner's meeting and some...shall we say sequestered pangs...somehow became reactivated. I called you originally to find out what you're about and where you're coming from. I didn't vote for you in the election, but I didn't vote at all...no offense. I am willing to get on the bandwagon just one more time here in the county. Your enthusiasm is contagious and I've decided I'll lend you my support and bring to bear whatever influence I may have."

"But you must prepare yourself for some purely illogical reactions to your ideas. I mean, if the public confuses craft for art, and if our officials can't even prepare a meaningful questionnaire -- those are your challenges. I can't help with public ignorance. But if you need someone to help 'bear the cross' I volunteer, sadistic as it probably is."

Barry and Beverly were near the door when the sound wheels on the gravel drive crunched to a halt. Car doors slammed and girls' laughter approached the front of the house. The door opened suddenly and three teenaged girls entered with a flutter of young female sounds and gestures that came to an abrupt halt when they realized that people were standing inside the door.

The tall, exuberant, lustrous, loud and dark one shouted, "Hi Mom." The other two shorter, quieter and lighter ones nodded a hello and passed on through into the house.

Mary said, "Beverly, this is my daughter Cynthia. She's on Barry's volleyball team."

"Our best blocker." Barry said with pride.

Cynthia was gazing at Barry with a soft light in her eyes that was an unmistakable sign of affection. Beverly remembered a crush she had had on one of her teachers back in Tennessee and smiled to herself at the bittersweet memory.

"I'll see you tomorrow afternoon, Mr. Hollister?" Cynthia said. After a moment of embarrassed hesitation she followed her friends into the kitchen. Instinctively, Beverly watched Barry's eyes for signs that he was following Cynthia's exit with more than a volleyball coach's interest in her form. Barry seemed totally disinterested.

Chapter Six

"Language is the house of the truth of Being." Heidegger

****

The valet brought his Olds around -- it had been a good car, no dents, just a few nicks from car doors parked too close. It would soon belong to Sharon and Bruce. Michael got in and headed uptown to Xavier's. As he was driving down 3rd avenue, he experienced some premature nostalgia about New York. He had clients in about 1/2 of the buildings he passed, well-satisfied clients at that 'cause he was good at what he did. Corporate law. Playing with words on documents. Maybe that was what he and Phillip had in common -- playing with words and covering asses. The difference between filing a brief and writing a philosophical treatise was, at least within the requirements of academia, very little.

What a great city, and I'm leaving it for the wild-wild-West, to help an artist deal with bureaucracy. "I must be crazy," he thought as he pulled into Xavier's parking lot, excited.

Felicity had known him well enough to know that this was to be no casual lunch. His taking her to lunch had always been an occasion to discuss this or that radical proposition. She had known from that last night in Acapulco, that his mind was taking one of those tangents the result of which she knew would be interesting, if not unsettling. But Michael had provided well -- never let her down. And she always kept that in mind. Although she was the last remaining Horowitz, she'd never had to tap into her trust and the kids were fixed for life. Michael had been a good provider. Actually, Michael had been the only suitor of whom she had no doubt he loved her for herself -- not because she was a steppingstone to something else. In fact when he asked her to marry him on that first trip to Europe, he didn't really know who the Horowitz's were. He was one of those clumsy but lovable Texans who exuded that kind of self-confidence -- that sort of frontier attitude -- that made them the butt of envy-lined remarks. His down-to-earthiness is what attracted her to him. As it turned out, he was absolutely great in bed -- her sensitive animal.

She had arrived just before Michael, and had had time to order some of Xavier's special escargot in mushroom caps -- the only reason they ever came here. No, on second thought, Xavier's beluga was the freshest in town. Michael slid in beside her just as she finished her first one.

"Hi, Fel. Great. Thanks for being prepared."

"Honey, you have to move pretty fast to get in front of me. So what's with you and Phillip?"

"Of course, I should've known you'd already know. You're right. I've got to help him. He's in Colorado, wanting to install what might be his last plastic work -- a sculpture just on the west side of the continental divide -- a LARGE sculpture. And he wants to put it on land under various jurisdictions among state federal and local bodies -- and he wants me to sort through the bureaucracy and get the various bodies to cooperate and approve of his plan. There's no money in it for me -- in fact my expenses will be mine to bear."

"What a surprise", Fel thought.

He paused while their waiter set down the escargot. "But I think I can't not do it. We don't need more money, and Sharon is going to continue to support my existing work here. I'll be in constant contact with her, here, but -- well -- I'm going to set up an office in Colorado in a couple of weeks. I've already given Sharron the go-ahead, and, Fel, whaddaya think?

"I knew something was on your mind, and I'm a little pissed that we didn't talk it through before you made up your mind, but since you've made up your mind already, I can only go along with you. Michael, you can do no wrong in my eyes. I love you forever, and only want what you want. You can do now, as you have always been able to do, whatever you want. You're good at what you do. I have no doubt that you love me and the kids. My only questions are how long will you be gone and how frequently can we see each other?"

"My question is, did you order some beluga? Fel, how can I tell you how much I love you for your understanding? I guess that's why we've stayed together so long. You can come to visit me as often as you want, and if that's not at least every couple of weeks, I'll hightail it back here to see you -- and the kids. What I'm going to be doing is temporary but it could take 3-4 months. I don't know right now. However long it takes, I've got to do it."

"I know, and it's this streak in you that I love -- and hate -- the most. You'll have my full support. But, I'll castrate you if you don't stay in touch. When're you leaving?"

"Within the next week or so."

"Ain't no fungus growin' under your feet, huh?"

He looked her straight in the eyes "Fell, I keep telling you you're no good at southern clichés. Its 'moss' not 'fungus'. Let's scarf down these snails, knock off another bottle of champagne and this beluga, and go home and see what happens next."

"You're so tactful..."

For the next 5 or 6 days after his lunch with Felicity, Michael, with Sharon's invaluable help, began ordering business affairs so he could make the move. They talked about a variety of communications technology that would enable him to stay in touch with New York: a desktop computer equipped with a fax/modem board, a laser printer, copier, and of course, his cell phone.

The move itself was going to be pretty much blind. He packed everything he could think he might need, but he had no idea where he was going to settle. All he knew that he was going to fly into Denver, lease a SUV, and head toward Summit County. His belongings were packed and ready to be shipped as soon as he gave the shippers an address.

Days flew by, and his time in the evenings with Felicity and the girls was particularly lucid. He knew he would miss them, and they knew they would miss him, but they were as understanding as possible. Or at least that was the picture they painted.

On the night before Michael's flight to Denver, Michelle, his 6-year-old, crawled up into his lap after dinner and asked why he was leaving them? "I'm not leaving you sweetie. I just have some work to do in Colorado for a while -- no different from trips I've taken before -- to Japan or San Francisco."

"But Dad, why are you packing so much stuff if you're only going on a business trip?"

With that, Felicity looked up at Michael to see how he would answer, and seeing that he would probably botch his response, she answered for him. "Daddy has a very important client who requires that he spend all his time on the project. He can't do the client a good job unless he moves to where the project is. Daddy can't stay here and do a good job there, so he's going to set up practice in Colorado for a short while. And anyway, we'll go visit him whenever we feel like it, and that will be fun 'cause we can go skiing and camping and all sorts of things.

"I'll come home whenever I can to make sure you're taking good care of Mom," Michael added.

Michelle knew that both her parents were being evasive, so she sighed resignedly, let the subject drop and kissed them goodnight.

Next morning, Michael kissed her before he headed out to La Guardia, and told her while she was sleeping that he would stay in close touch and that he loved her.

Felicity drove him to the airport. While the conversation was banal, she couldn't help but feel that this departure was different from all the others she'd experienced over the past 15 years. The kiss at the terminal was meaningful, but she knew Michael's mind was on the adventure he was about to undertake.

"Call me as soon as you get settled, wherever, sweetheart."

"You know I will. And Fel, thanks again for your understanding and support. I'll stay in close touch. You should check into the possibility of commuter fares to Denver. Maybe there's some sort of ticket you can buy that gives you unlimited flights for a set price. Whatever, I want you to feel free to come out whenever you want to. And I'll do the same. I love you more than you know."

Michael turned, walked through the turnstiles, took a deep breath, and got mentally prepared for what he remembered Heidegger called "openness" to a situation. He was going to live this experience as if viewing a piece of art for the first time.

He was prepared to spend the four-hour flight to Denver in thought. But instead, he was so exhausted from the anxiety of the past couple of weeks that he fell asleep as soon as he fastened his seatbelt.

Next thing he knew the plane was landing in Denver, and he was off on an adventure, the likes of which he hadn't given himself the possibility to encounter for -- for too long to remember.

He picked up the lease SUV, loaded his luggage, and headed west on highway 70. Jesus, it was beautiful. He'd had several business deals in Denver over the past few years, but on all those trips, it was fly-in, consult, and fly back to New York. He could see the mountains from this or that 15th Street office building in Denver, but he'd never taken time to follow his urge to drive up into them. This time, his business was not in Denver, but in the mountains, and his attitude was "open" as he headed west.

It was just after noon. The sun's reflection on traces of snow at the upper elevations, cameoed by magnificent dark green spruce and pine trees along the way, was nostalgically breathtaking.

About 10 miles out of Denver, the Wagoner began struggling against the ascending elevation. Foothills first, then, after passing the Buffalo Herd overlook at Genesee, the hills became the eastern slope of the Rockies, and the scenery passed from rolling to acute. Idaho Springs, with antiquated mines on both sides of the highway, passed by the windshield to the side windows and into the rear-view mirror quicker than Michael wanted. He was getting hungry, and decided to pull off at the next possible spot for something to eat. In a few more twisting, ascending miles, signs for Georgetown inclined him not to miss the exit. Sure enough, in a few more minutes, the exit to Georgetown beckoned him.

Taking the exit, at first he saw only some gas stations and fast food restaurant signs. But once he was off the highway, he could see that Georgetown had more to offer. Heading southwest off the main route, there was actually an old Victorian mining town snuggled into the intersection of two of the craggy mountains. There was still a main street there, and he parked the Wagoneer at the first available space.

He was exhausted from the day-long trip. In less than a block, he came upon the Adam's Hotel and Restaurant. The menu was posted at the entrance included Prime Rib, Steaks, Trout, some Mexican entrees, Hamburgers, and the like. He looked through the stained-glass window, saw an appealing atmosphere, and went in. It was about 1:30 p.m.

The place was almost empty; a couple of people having drinks in one of the booths, and another few guys at the bar. Although a sign said, "please wait to be seated" he knew there was no hostess, so he sauntered over to the bar, sat down, and fairly quickly an efficient bartendress asked for his order.

"Any chance of getting something to eat?"

She glanced at her watch, mostly out of habit, and said, "Sure, wanna see a menu?"

"No, just give me a Coors, and tell me what you have. I've been traveling all day, and I'm hungry and thirsty."

"Where're ya from" as she gave him a lunch menu.

"New York."

"Really?"

"Yeh. Any burgers possible?"

"Sure. Buffalo burgers. How d'ya want it?"

"Rare."

"Buffalo is moist anyway and usually better medium or well."

"Let me have a buffalo burger cooked the usually best way."

"It'll be just a few minutes."

She went over to the window between the bar and kitchen, placed his order and returned. "What's a New Yorker doing in Georgetown on a Wednesday in October?"

"To be honest, ordering a buffalo burger and looking for a place to rent. D'ya know of anything?"

"Well this is a hotel, ya know, and if it's too expensive, there's the Comfort Inn back down on the service road."

"No, I mean something nice to rent for several months."

"Really. Why'd you want to stay in Georgetown for several months?"

"Mostly business."

"What kind of business -- oh, sorry, excuse me for prying. Just trying to make conversation."

"That's ok. Thanks for the concern. Really, I need a nice 2-3 bedroom home to rent for a few months. Know where I could find one?

"I don't, but Alice Emerson over there at that booth knows all about that stuff. She owns the Century 21 real estate."

"Where is hotel registration?" deciding instantly to stay here until he got the lay of the land.

"Oh, just up those stairs."

"I'll be back in a minute."

He went up to hotel registration while his burger was being prepared, registered for a room, and went back to the restaurant. He inhaled his burger, which was moist and good well done, and stopped over at the booth where the bartendress told him Alice, the real estate broker, sat.

"Excuse me. My name's Michael. The waitress told me you're a realtor, and I'm looking for a place to lease for the next few months. Can you help?"

"I'm Alice Emerson, call me Allie. Pleased to meet you. What kind of place are you looking for, and how much can you pay?"

"Well, I'm an attorney, and I will be working out of the house, so I probably need a three-bedroom home. I guess I can pay what the market demands. The question is, "are there any homes for lease around here?"

"Sure, but, we're headed into ski season, and prices are usually quoted for a week -- short term rentals, not for several months. A typical home will rent for $7-800 per week."

For Michael, this didn't sound like much since his Manhattan condominium cost him $7,000 a month.

"I can pay around that, but I'd think if I wanted a rental for several weeks -- or months, that I could get it for less than $500 a week." Michael couldn't suppress his innate negotiating bent.

"True. How long did you need the lease? The minimum would be six months."

"That's fine. Do you have anything?"

"There're a couple of possibilities. The Brown house is up just at the southwest edge of town. It's a nice, old Victorian home furnished with antiques -- they need a $1,000 security deposit. And the Barrett lodge is over on the river. It's a log structure, works great as a ski lodge for a large family during ski season -- big moss-rock fireplace, its own well and septic system. The Brown house could be had for about $1,200 a month, and the Barrett lodge for about $1,900."

"When could I see them?"

"How about tomorrow afternoon?"

"I have an appointment then. Could I see them now?"

"I have to show a couple of condominiums this afternoon, but I guess I could show you these places late this evening, say, 6:30."

"OK. Where do I meet you?"

"My office, just across the street. I'll be there between 6:30 and 7:00. Are you prepared to put down a deposit and the first month's rent if you like one of them?"

"Yes, if you'll take either an out of town check or American Express for payment. I just pulled into town today and haven't opened a bank account. By the way, where is the bank?"

"1st National, Georgetown, is two blocks over."

"Thanks Allie. See you this evening."

Michael went back to his car, drove it around to the hotel parking lot, got his luggage, and moved into the room he'd rented for a week. As soon as he got unpacked, he went over to the bank, opened up an account with a wire transfer from New York, walked around town for a while to get the lay of the land. Nice town. Quaint, mining history, quite a few pseudo-galleries filled mostly with crafts by locals. A hardware store, 5-6 dining establishments, two hotels in addition to the Adams, a dozen or so real estate and insurance offices, a mountaineering-backpacking-cross-country skiing shops, a couple of downhill ski-rental shops, 8-9 bars, and the like. At 6:15 he headed over to Alice's Century 21 office across the street.

She was there, but preoccupied with writing a contract, apparently with one of the buyers she showed condos to this afternoon. She barely acknowledged his presence, and motioned for him to sit in the anteroom.

"Real estate people" Michael thought, "are the same everywhere. Close! Close! Close! And when that's over, try to close another." Alice had a good line of sales-person's bullshit, had obviously been through Century 21's video training program, and was affably efficient at her work.

About 20 minutes later, the new condo owners left, contracts in hand and dreams in heart, and Alice appeared.

"Thanks for waiting -- just closed a deal. Let me buy ya a drink before we go looking at those homes?"

"Sure. I've nothing else to do. My time's yours."

Alice was perfunctory, in her late 50's, confident, and apparently fairly successful. She put the phones on answering service, turned off typewriters and computers, left the entry light on, and locked up as they left. Without any words, she steered him back over to the Adams bar and ordered a double scotch for herself. Michael ordered the same.

"So" she asked after gulping down 1/2 her drink "what's a New York attorney doing in Georgetown, Colorado?"

"You're the second person that's asked that in the last few hours. Does it really make a difference? Oh well, I've a client who needs some help dealing with the various branches of government as they relate to a piece of land just the other side of Eisenhower tunnel, on Highway 70."

Alice almost choked on her drink. "Really? A land sale?" She seemed more curious than she let on as she said it.

"No, probably just use -- in whatever form. I really don't have many details just now. Won't know until after tomorrow what it is I'm up against. But this client is a long-time relationship, and he just told me to get out here and set up shop. I still have clients back in New York to keep up with, but I suspect most of my efforts will be spent here, dabbling in and among the various bureaucracies."

"Ever been out here before?"

"Yeah. Spent several summers here when we -- this client and me -- were in graduate school. He more or less remained, and I sought fortune and fame in the big city. Yeah. I know the countryside fairly well for a 'feriner'."

"Do you ski?"

"Not really -- no more nor less than the next turkey. I really loved the Rockies for the summers more than the winters."

Alice downed the remainder of her drink, looked at her watch, and suggested they head out. She wanted more information about the tunnel land, but didn't, for now at least, inquire further. Michael knew Allie had qualified him enough to know he wasn't a transient ski bum. He paid the tab, and they got into Allie's Subaru and headed to the Brown house.

It was as she described it, Victorian, antiques, very nice. Then they went to the Barrett lodge-rustic, on the river, large.

After seeing both of the possibilities, there was no doubt which Michael preferred -- the Barrett lodge, so he requested that Alice attend to the details, and draw up a six-month lease. He left her a check for $1,000 to indicate his seriousness. She said she'd get in touch with him tomorrow or the next day. Michael gave her his cell phone number, retired to his room and literally passed out from exhaustion at having been at it for almost 20 hours. He'd call Fel first thing in the morning. It was already 1:15 am, New York time.

****

At her house, Beverly was puttering around with dinner, all the while anxious to hear how Barry's first encounter with the commissioners and county government players had gone. She knew Barry would be anxious to have someone to discuss it with and she'd promised to cook one of her specialties -- Lasagna.

Dressed in a light gray cotton sweater and roomy old jeans she was feeling very gentle and homey watching out the kitchen window for Barry to turn into the driveway. She was trying to evade any feeling of warmth and security in this situation but it felt so good she stopped trying for tonight. She could face realities tomorrow.

The night was cold, and frozen humidity created sparkles in the headlights of Barry's BMW as he turned up the drive. Beverly felt a flush of anticipation come to her shoulders and face. There was a sense of serenity in the silence of the darkness. Barry approached the house framed by a clear night. A million stars twinkled against the pure black sky. He knocked on the door. She yelled for him to come on in and when he peered past the doorway she was in the kitchen, bent over putting the French bread in the oven. She knew her soft jeans were revealing the well-tuned shape her behind. Bathed in the warm light of the kitchen she made herself lusty and beautiful in Barry's eyes.

Beverly closed the oven, turned around, walked over to Barry. Without saying anything they embraced for a long time. A giant hug. Her perfume and aroma of emerging sexual arousal mingled with the smell of his body and tobacco. She let herself wilt into his strength and they just stood quietly in the kitchen, entwined. As his hand crept underneath the backside of her sweater she was happy of her decision to leave off a bra. His excited hand moved smoothly down her spine, past the waistband of her trousers, and rested with his strong fingers just above her tailbone.

She pressed her hips into his and could feel his presence asserting itself. Motionless and dizzy for an instant she was feeling things she'd not felt since her first dates with Daniel. For a moment she was going to forget dinner and go straight for the bed but she reminded herself that there was time and Lasagna.

Finally, she leaned back and said "Glad you're here Barry. Hope you like Italian. I've cooked some really great Lasagna."

Barry caught his breath and followed her lead. "Love it. And I've brought some wine. The selection at the liquor store was sparse, but they finally came up with a nice Bardolino." Barry took some things from a bag by the door. "Want some now?"

"Sure. There're some wine glasses in that cabinet above the toaster."

Barry got the glasses, opened and poured the wine, and handed a glass to Beverly. "Ciao." he said, and they toasted the occasion.

She smiled at his worldliness, went back over to the stove and began preparing their plates. He crossed to the stereo. When Beverly heard piano music emerging from the speakers she knew it wasn't Jerry Lee Lewis or Professor Longhair so she figured Barry had brought music with him.

"It's Rachmaninoff's Second Piano Concerto." He called above the music and sat down at the dining room table.

As the second movement of the concerto began, Barry couldn't keep from getting up from the table and going over to the stereo. Both his hands were cupped over the headset, and when Beverly walked in from the kitchen, he motioned her over, placed the earphones on her head, and turned up the volume. She stood there for a minute. The unfamiliar music played directly on her emotions.

She felt that Van Cliburn's quick and adroit fingers were running over her body.

When the second movement ended in its pastoral image Barry took back the headphones. He had a look of admiration and enjoyment that she wished she could understand. He held her head in his hands and placed a soft kiss on her forehead.

"Pure romanticism." Barry said. "Utter nostalgia, raw feeling. I fell in love with this when I saw the old British film 'Brief Encounter' during a film fest in New Haven."

Beverly broke loose from Barry, went to the kitchen and brought dinner to the table. She knew the lasagna would have to compete with Rachmaninoff for Barry's sensual pleasure but she felt good about its chances. Beverly's lasagna approached perfection.

As they sat down, the final movement was at its crescendo. They both felt a little warmth from the wine and a lot of warmth from the music. Without words, Beverly filled their plates, sat down, and they listened to the music end.

After a considerate silence Beverly said, "How was the meeting tonight?"

"About what I expected, but I might have made an ass of myself. They went through their normal reports, and when new business was called for, I asked about the possibility of an Arts Committee. They heard my requisition and a few ass holes made some jokes about it. By-and-large they were polite but wrote me off as a new commissioner, saying they were operating within budget constraints, and with that, the discussion was ended.

"I could've told you that."

Beverly filled him in on the various players and what she knew of their roles in the community as they ate. Then she could stand no more small talk and delay. The food had Barry's attention but she wanted the rest of him. Amidst some comment from his role as a new commissioner, she got up from her chair, walked around to his side of the table, and planted a really deep kiss on him. Their kiss was long, wet and mutually appreciative. Her juices were flowing into her brain so forcefully that she began to lose control. This is how life ought to be spent, she thought.

Barry responded by pulling her body down into his lap and again they just embraced -- long and hard.

Beverly said they could have dessert anytime, and with that, they headed to her bedroom.

Screw Rachmaninoff, Beverly thought. This is raw romanticism that we'll both remember forever. She lay with her head on Barry's shoulder listening to his heartbeat return to normal.

After a long ambrosial pause, Beverly felt Barry's muscles tighten back to alertness as his mind returned to the commissioners meeting. "When I mentioned an art commission," He said, "some of them tried to make jokes about the idea. I thought they were sharper than that."

"You mean their jokes weren't funny?" Beverly asked.

"They didn't listen to what I was saying about art." Barry persisted.

"What made you think of art?"

"I don't know. It was just as far as I could get from septic maintenance. I wanted to make something happen. I've had a lot of time to think about it."

"You said you've traveled a lot." Beverly really didn't know a many of the details of Barry's life.

"I guess I've told you, after my MBA at Yale I took off to Europe for almost six months. Spent most of August on the French Riviera."

He gave Beverly's a squeeze and she pushed his hand away in mock resentment. "There's not a more beautiful place to be in August than Cannes or St. Tropez. In September I went to Paris and became enthralled at everything related to fashion and fashion shows -- weird people whose whole way of life is adornment."

"Isn't that exclusive?"

"My family name carried just enough clout to gain admittance to some of the runway shows. The cuisine in Paris was the best in the world, save perhaps, New Orleans. I enjoyed November in Barcelona, took untold numbers of rolls of film at the Daliesque sculpture. Then I took off to Flaine, Les Carroz and Chamonix for the winter holidays. I learned to ski. Finally in late February, I decided to spend the remainder of the winter at my folk's place out here in Summit County.

"Did you find a girl out here." Beverly said. Trying to find out something else about him without interrupting his reverie.

"Not till now. Not since Europe. My idea of the typical woman in Summit is one who wears no make-up, has shoulder length mousy-brown hair, has a an ass and legs like a sumo-wrestler, has tenure of 1.78 years, she's here to get out of her system that urge she'd had in high-school to express her female identity by screwing as much as the boys, likely has a 2-3 year-old child from a failed marriage to a construction worker, has skin like my old baseball glove, and comports herself toward men, especially non-bearded, well-dressed, businessmen, as if raising her child alone and in poverty is a virtue."

Beverly laughed, convulsively, out loud.

"I read the local newspapers," he continued, "did some work around my parent's cabin, skied and fished. I didn't want to be just a tourist. I wanted people to think of me as part of the community. I used to be a pretty good volleyball player and I volunteered to coach for the youth center. They let me build a team for the Mountain Girls League."

"I'll bet all the girls think you're cute." Beverly teased.

"I am cute," Barry replied, "but I'm also a professional.

"You're a volunteer." Beverly insisted.

Barry persisted in finishing his story. "One day I noticed in the paper that there was soon to be a county commissioner election due to the death of one of the former commissioners."

"That was old Hank Abrams." Beverly elaborated. "It was hard to tell if he was alive before he died."

"Somewhat out of boredom, somewhat out of curiosity, but mostly out of vanity, I decided I'd run for the office."

Beverly was trying to be thoughtful. "Don't you have to know everybody to get elected?"

"I had a plan. I met one or two of the commissioners at some of those pre-ski-season chamber of commerce mixers that admitted a mixture of politicians and persons vying for permanent -- as opposed to seasonal -- employment attend. Surprisingly enough, the politicos had their shit together pretty well. I decided I'd base my meager campaign strategy on the platform that "new blood" was needed in the commission. So I spent the next several weeks being gregarious -- against my druthers -- intentionally meeting local businessmen, learning their concerns. Then, as it turned out, no one else ran for the open seat, so here I am. Your dedicated public servant, at least for the last 28 months of a deceased commissioner's term."

Beverly returned to the original topic. "So now you're going to become the arts czar."

"This is all related. From the love of beautiful breasts I came to love beauty itself. I experienced the best food, the finest clothes then the highest art. It was all art. Art is the best of anything. After my first winter here, I got interested in fly-fishing, so I stayed the summer. Then I learned to tie my own flies so the experience could be the best. There's hardly a better feeling than landing a sixteen incher on one of the elk-hair caddis I've tied myself. For the class-A fisherman, it isn't which fly is used, but how it's tied. But then for some of the real 'salts', it doesn't even matter which fly is used but how it's presented. All is a matter of presentation, of quality or style. It's a matter of art.

"But you see what I'm saying. My family's business has always been business but I've been learning that I'm attracted to situations where the business is art. I don't know if there's any power in the county commission but I've got twenty-eight months to try to use it in some way. I need to do something to make a difference."

Beverly was thinking how strangely her life was merging with Barry's. This was a spiritual sign or at least a remarkable coincidence.

"Let me tell you what happened today." Beverly said. She took a deep breath. "I made my break with Andrew clear and permanent."

"You said you were going to do that. Are you OK?"

"I'm OK now but I was pretty stressed out. I went through the motions of my job for the rest of the afternoon and by 6 o'clock when I locked up the store, I needed a place to think. There were a couple more hours of daylight so I went home and put Brownie in the back seat of the Toyota, and headed out to the Swan River road. Where the road turns to gravel the Swan River runs really so slow over those boulders."

"That was strip mined in the early 20's." Barry interjected.

"I think so but now the river is always clear and blue. Its gurgles and hisses were calling to Brownie and he whined in the back seat for me to stop. Brownie's getting old and I had tears in my eyes thinking about the day I would lose him that chased away the tears from thinking about Andrew.

"I ignored Brownie's whining and let my mind wander away from today's problems. When I was a girl I thought my imperfection made me unhappy and I wanted god to punish me so I could deserve to be happy. Maybe now I realize how much I'm on my own. Nobody's going to fix anything for me. And now that I've realized it, the real challenge of being something special sits there, mocking me, daring me to do something about it. I used to think I'd make a difference. Now, it's all I can do to keep from being swept away.

"I turned up the road to the north fork of the Swan River, about five miles north of town. I parked the Toyota, and Brownie and I headed up a trail we'd never been on before. There's already a lot of snow in the shaded areas. In some cases it's almost a foot deep but the stream is low in late October so we walked as much as possible along the stream. In some spots it's barely flowing. It's deep in other places where there are pools left by that giant runoff we had last spring. Brownie went chasing after small brown trout that were playing in the pools.

"About a mile up the creek we saw a cabin sitting up away from the bank. I climbed up to check it out. It looked run down but it had lots of cordwood stacked around under the eaves so I knew somebody lived there. I didn't want to be hanging around somebody's house so I turned back to the creek but Brownie was already circling around to the back. I was calling to Brownie but he can be a disobedient shit sometime. Then I saw a bearded man's face in the window. It was distorted in the shadows and looked horrible.

The hair went up on the back of my neck. I was really scared and I started to run. I knew Brownie would catch up. Then the man came to the door and I stopped. He wasn't a monster. He was just a big guy with a white beard and an old plaid shirt. I should know better than to trust a strange man. A lot of guys still think that if a woman's out wandering around alone she deserves whatever happens to her but there was so much peace and contentment in his eyes I didn't think he could hurt me. Then, Brownie came to the door. He'd already found his way in from the back and I knew if Brownie liked the guy he was OK."

"Where is Brownie?" Barry wondered.

"I put him out. If he was inside a little while ago he'd have stuck his cold nose in your butt at a really bad moment."

"I went up and sat on the porch and just talked to the guy. With his big white beard I couldn't tell if he was fifty years old or a hundred. He said he'd been living up there in that log cabin that was, according to him, constructed in 1905."

"How would he know?" Barry asked.

"He'd been homesteading there since 1977. Some of the cabin was really old. Some of the boards on the porch looked new. I asked him about electricity - he had none, used lanterns for light. I asked him about water - he drank from the stream, never in 12 years having got lamblia giardia. He had 8-10 cords of wood cut and stacked by the cabin for heat. He hadn't gone hunting this year, 'cause he still had meat left over from last year.

I couldn't think of much to talk about so I asked him if the birds and squirrels came into his cabin. He said they were welcome in the cabin depending mostly on his mood. Their interested in him depended mostly on the quantity and quality of his scraps.

I told him I envied his life-style. He asked me if that was my Toyota parked a few miles back down the road? I thought may be that meant he wanted me to go.

There wasn't much else to talk about. I called Brownie and started to head back down the path. He smiled and asked me to come back and visit if I wanted to. I told him I would but I knew he wouldn't care if I didn't. I realized he was a hermit. I had heard about hermits living out here but I'd never actually seen one."

"I guess not being seen is what makes a hermit." Barry added.

"But he was a real one; long beard and the whole thing. I couldn't think how to ask him why he was living out there alone but everything about his life seemed to make him happy. From what I could see, I was thinking I'd trade my life for his in a heartbeat. Or would I? It was not deja vu 'cause I wasn't a hermit. Yet! But he made me think that I could find my own way if I put my heart to it. St. Paul taught us that there's a variety of gifts but always the same spirit; there are all sorts of service to be done but always to the same Lord. We all work in different ways but it's the same God who's working in all of us."

Barry said. "I'm not much of a Bible reader."

"It's not just a Bible thing." Beverly continued. "God is whatever you think is most real. Maybe God is just a word. Like you said art wasn't just the stuff under glass in the museum but was whatever was best."

"So you're not only a beautiful woman who mixes great Lasagna with explosive sex." Barry said. "You're also a philosopher."

"Not really." Beverly said. Missing Barry's irony. "I grew up with contempt and regret for my sins. I read a lot of stuff for really personal reasons when I was a kid. I had to be careful though. The deep water Baptists in Tennessee would wonder why any saved person would read the Catholic Saints."

"They've got a point." Barry said. "The boys from St. Luke's I knew on the playground never were interested in love or charity. They were usually looking to kick someone's ass."

"I read St. Catherine. She said one person would be given charity as a primary virtue, another would get justice, somebody else humility or maybe a lively faith or prudence or patience or courage. You see each of us gets a virtue so we're dependent on one another and each of us can be God's minister. The soul is most at ease with that virtue which has been made primarily for her. I just need to find out what my virtue is.

"Following Brownie, I trekked back down the path to the car. The meeting with the hermit was more than chance. I've always thought my life was more than chance. Dad had told me when I was a teenager that "Ya get out what ya put in". He wanted me to make a difference. God he was pissed when I ran off with Daniel. My dad died before I ever went back to visit. He was a great guy, and just now I really miss him."

Tears came back into Beverly's eyes. Barry pulled her closer and brushed them from her cheek as they fell.

"So you're looking for a special virtue?" He asked. "Is there anything I can do to help?" Barry's stroking of Beverly's cheeks was turning into a general caress of the rest of her body.

"That was my point." Beverly replied. "You're looking for an answer in your Arts Commission. I was thinking maybe I could help. Oh, maybe on a related note, Andrew told me some guy was in his office recently -- a guy who ostensibly was representing some New York artist who wanted to put sculpture up at the Eisenhower Tunnel."

"Interesting" Barry's replied. "Maybe there is a possibility for Art in Summit County."

"Let me know if there's any way I can help."

Chapter Seven

"And if you gaze long enough into an abyss, the abyss will gaze back into you." Nietzsche

****

Michael woke up the next morning at the Adams in Georgetown. It took him a couple of minutes to realize where he was and what he was doing. He went down to the restaurant, ordered coffee, and called Sharon from his cell phone – at least there was service here. "Any messages?"

"Where are you?"

"In Georgetown, Colorado. Shar, its friggin' beautiful here in the mountains. Lots of good memories. I've rented a home that I should move into in a few days. Any messages?

"Yea. Theo Boudreaux called and said they couldn't meet you today. Said they were en route to Coon Hill." Michael could hear Sharon turning to her notes. "He said you'd know what he was talking about. They were going to be in touch with a "Jake" in Silverthorne, but something about that has gone wrong. They'll get in touch. It'll be probably in two or three more days before they can meet you. Mr. Boudreaux told me to give you this name. Do you have a pen? Andrew Wolltrip, of the Summit County Commissioner's Office. Wolltrip was also going to call Lem in Wyoming, but that's screwed. He needs a follow up right away. Said that on your way over to Wolltrip's office, you'd go through Eisenhower Tunnel and that you should notice the piece of empty land just off to the right as you exited the tunnel headed west. By the way, your computer should arrive in a few days. Call me once it's there and I'll walk you through setting it up with the modem."

"You have Wolltrip's phone number?"

"No, but I'll get it for you. Where'll you be the next hour or so?"

"Here at the Adams. Call when you have it. Anything else?"

"No, I let all the folks involved with the AMAX deal know your position. They're thinking!"

"Thinking, huh. I hope they don't hurt themselves. Oh well. Good. O.k. Talk to ya later."

Michael went back into the restaurant, ate breakfast, and went back to his room to call Felicity.

"Hello, Fel, how's things?"

"Oh Michael, it's so good to hear your voice. I've not had a moment when I wasn't thinking of you. The girls? Ok, they're at school and I'm having lunch with Marcia. Tell me what's going on there."

"I'm at the Adams Hotel in Georgetown. I'll be here another couple of days, then I'm moving into a house I've rented. Nice place. You'll like it when you come to visit. I'm going to call on one of the players in the Summit county commissioner's office this afternoon. Haven't met with Philip and TBoy yet, they're somewhere en route to a camping spot near Eisenhower tunnel. I think I'll be in touch with them in a day or two. Have you had a chance to learn about commuter fares?"

"No, not yet, but I will. Thought you needed to get well settled in before I make any plans to visit. You remember don't you that we're supposed to visit my folks in Connecticut for Thanksgiving. Do you still plan to go? If not, we should let Elsa know."

"Sure, I still plan for us to go. I wouldn't miss Thanksgiving with you and your family-- you know that."

"I wasn't sure."

"Come on Fel, I'm just on business here. Nothing has changed. Anything else?"

"No, only that I miss you, and so do the girls. Call them after school as soon as you can."

"You know I will. I love you too, Fel. Take care."

Michael went back to his room. The light on the phone was blinking, so he called the front desk and got a message from Sharon that simply said Andrew Wolltrip, 970-453-1212. He dialed the number.

"Mr. Wolltrip, please."

"Just a minute. Who's calling?"

This is Michael Lovell. I'm calling on behalf of Philip Alathon."

After a couple of minutes

"This is Andrew Wolltrip, how can I help?"

"I'm Michael Lovell and I represent an artist named Philip Alathon. A few weeks ago you met with Theodore Boudreaux about Mr. Alathon's desire to put a sculpture up at Eisenhower tunnel. You were to get back to them, and…"

"I tried to call the number they gave me, in Wyoming I think it was, but the person who answered was very uncooperative..."

"I know, that's why they asked me to call. They're in the process of moving over here from Wyoming, and they've asked me to get in touch with you. I'm an attorney -- former schoolmate of Mr. Alathon's -- and they want me to help them work through whatever is required to determine the possibility of bringing this sculpture to fruition. I wonder if you could meet with me within the next day or so?"

"I was thinking about that sculpture proposal yesterday." Andrew Wolltrip said enthusiastically. In fact I've got somebody from the county commission that I want you to meet. Let me see what I can set up but we could meet, tentatively, at 4:30 this afternoon."

Michael offered his thanks to Andrew Wolltrip and hung up. He was surprised to find such a cooperative city employee. He realized he'd become jaded by life in New York. Andrew Wolltrip was what small town life was all about---openness, cooperation, and old-fashioned service.

He headed over to Alice's office to sign a lease on Barrett lodge. A note on the door instructed him to meet her at the house, so he decided to walk the mile or so through downtown Georgetown. Passing antique shops, craft galleries, bars, and a variety store he tried to imagine an argument to convince the owners of these businesses that what they really needed in their budget was a major work of modern art. He wanted a point of focus for his upcoming meeting with Wolltrip and but was too excited about the lease he was about to enter into. Besides, he surmised, he could think about that conversation while driving the forty-five minutes or so over to the commissioner's office.

As he approached the house, his pace quickened. He was excited about the new abode. Stream flowing right beyond the balcony, lots of large windows. Alice was there on the balcony waiting for him. He could see her there as he approached.

"Alice, how's things?

"Couldn't be better Michael. How've you been?" Alice's words were cheerful but her expression and posture told a different story.

They exchanged pleasantries and Michael signed the lease quickly. He could tell she had something else on her mind and wanted to let her go as soon as possible. Alice told him to send his check directly to the Barrett's address in Houston. She reminded him to get the utilities changed into his name -- told him to expect pretty high utility bills -- gave him the names of a couple of firewood dealers, handed him the key and wished him luck. She was so perfunctory.

"Let me know if I can be of any further help."

"You've been a great help already. By the way, is this place for sale?"

"I don't think so, why?"

"Oh, just wondering. Who knows? I think this place could grow on me. Don't know what might happen after I've completed my work here. I've had thoughts about living in the mountains ever since graduate school. And my family -- I have two preteen daughters -- likes to ski."

"I'll find out if you want. How's your work going, by the way."

"Oh, just getting started. Again thanks, Alice, for your help. Oh, while we're talking about real estate, do you have any way of knowing who owns the land up around the west end of the tunnel?"

"No, but..." Alice paused as if making up her mind about something, you told me you wanted to do something with that piece of land."

"Who've you been talking to?"

"Don't you know a woman in town named Darcy?"

"I just got here."

"Darcy's a barkeeper at Tony's. She called to tell me about your friend. She wanted me to help him with this if I could. I wasn't supposed to tell you." Alice was agitated.

"Don't worry about it." Michael said. "Philip Alathon is famous in some circles and he's well known to quite a few bartenders. I just want to know how she found out he's up here. I don't even know exactly where he is."

"If I was his lawyer I'd keep him away from that tunnel."

Michael thought this was a curious thing to say. "I know it's going to be a tangled mess but Philip has a way of cutting through bullshit."

"I'm not worried about the red tape." Alice was grim and serious. "Eisenhower Tunnel has a history that a lot of people in this town like to keep quiet. I don't want to get mixed up in it again but I like you and I wanted to warn you."

After Alice drove off, Michael went inside, sat down on the chair in the living room. All places harbor secrets, he thought. To make anything happen one has to shine light into places that someone else wants to keep dark. Michael tried to imagine how his life here would be. He decided he'd set up his desk over in front of the large plate glass window in the den, looking out over the stream. There was an old wooden rocking chair there that would be perfect for -- for sitting and thinking. He'd been almost glued to a rocking chair for most of his graduate work and he was feeling warmed by the nostalgia. He toured the house and examined the closets and kitchen. Everything was well stocked. It even had a washer/dryer. He was pleased. After an hour or so, he locked the place up, trekked back to the hotel, got his car and headed over to his meeting with Wolltrip.

It was a little over ten miles up to the tunnel, an ascent of about 2,500 feet. Michael slowed as he came out the nether end. As T-Boy had described it, there was a large parcel of land just off to the north which was apparently unused. There was a shed --

probably a maintenance warehouse -- tucked back up to the east of the parcel, but it was barely noticeable. Christ, they're a lot of highway signs up here. Hardly seems necessary, he thought as he watched the several uniformed tunnel personnel scurry about.

As the Wagoneer descended down past what he would later learn was Hamilton Gulch, into the Tenderfoot mountain valley he began to think about the levels of bureaucracy that would need to be pierced. Passing through Silverthorne, he stopped and picked up a USGS quad map of the area from the Forest Service office, then headed toward the county commissioner's office. It was about 4:00 p.m., and the drive over the continental divide had the effect of purging his soul. It had been a long time since he had been in the mountains, and he instantly grasped Philip's appreciation of their awesome power over the imagination.

He parked outside the county offices, and went inside, following the signs to the commissioner's offices. He purposely hadn't brought a briefcase, thinking it to be too overbearing in a rural community setting. A plain woman of indeterminate age sat at a desk behind the nameplate 'Darlene Scruggs'.

"May I help you, sir?"

"My name's Michael Lovell, and I have an appointment with Mr. Wolltrip."

Darlene glanced up at the wall clock. "Mr. Wolltrip is expecting you, but he's tied up at the moment. Won't you have a seat?"

Michael was a few minutes early and he assumed that, like any good secretary, Darlene wanted to make the stranger think her boss' time was important. The lordly Mr. Wolltrip was probably sitting behind the door scratching his balls and staring at the furniture so Michael settled into assessing the decor side on his side of the door. The office was a little sparse, but Felicity would call that a hard-edged Modernist look. A government office should look clean and efficient. He looked around, the only magazines related to highway maintenance and childcare advice. So he just sat and resisted the temptation to scratch.

The door opened and a well-dressed young man came in. He was obviously the owner or son of the owner of an expensive mountain vacation property. He had born to win written all over him. Michael truly resented this kind of privileged pretty boy when he was growing up in Texas but he had learned that he could kick his ass on the football field or a New York boardroom and got over it. That sharp look of success made a good man to have up front on a negotiating team.

"Good afternoon, Darlene." The newcomer said.

Darlene buzzed the inner office. "Mr. Wolltrip," she announced. "Mr. Lovell and Mr. Hollister are here to see you."

The door opened immediately and Andrew Wolltrip emerged. Smiling to Michael he said, "Michael Lovell may I introduce you to Barry Hollister. I believe you two will have a lot in common."

Michael shook Barry's hand and followed Andrew into his office. In contrast to the reception area, the inner office reminded Michael of an Oriental movie set.

Andrew motioned his visitors to a wicker sofa in the corner and drew up a chair from the center of the room for himself. He sat grasping the unusually high arms of the strange metal chair so that his elbows pointed left and right almost level with his chin. He leaned back and forth over the sides of the chair and looked down as if from a great height to the Persian carpet below. He said, apropos of nothing, "Can you see a stain on this carpet? I'll have to get Darlene to get it cleaned immediately."

Neither of the visitors offered an opinion on the stain so Andrew opened the conversation about Philip's sculpture. "I'm not sure where to start, but I assume we all have an interest in the arts or we wouldn't be here." He turned to Barry. "Barry, as I mentioned on the phone, Michael represents an artist who has a very interesting idea to erect a monument on public land at Eisenhower Tunnel. And I have here the minutes of the last board meeting. Michael, you might find Barry's comments about an Arts program of some value." Andrew handed Michael the first document from the top of an enormous stack of paper.

He continued talking and passing documents. "Let me show you what I've been able to do so far. It's quite a strange request but I did gather some information, which I'm pleased to relay to you. First of all, the piece of land in question is recorded at the county clerk's office. Here's the reception number. You will probably want to review these restrictions, encumbrances, easements and ownership there. I also photocopied all the relevant title information on the land parcel up on the continental divide. As could be expected, there were over twenty pages of legalese relating to those particular parcels."

Michael was amazed, "I'm impressed with your research." He said sincerely. "It will save me some time."

"You're quite welcome. We are here to serve. In my opinion, the most important element of your search would reveal that the state of Colorado owns easements across the land. And the federal highway department is involved insofar as they approve funds to the state for maintenance. The state sort of subcontracts to the county for maintenance support. I'm not sure where you should begin, but I can refer you to Jim Bagnold, here in our office. Jim is in charge of our Road and Bridge department. And Harry Bain is in charge of land use. Here are their phone numbers. They can probably at least get you headed in the right direction, if there is a "right" direction for your pursuit. Oh, yes. At some point you might need to talk with Sam Cummings over at inter-government relations. He knows his way around pretty well. The more people you can get involved with this the better. And that brings us to Barry. I suppose you'll need community involvement with a public arts project and he's the man to organize it for you."

"Again, your preparation is pretty awesome." Michael repeated. He turned to Barry. "I really appreciate your help."

Barry was completely unprepared and appeared confused. He said to Andrew, "I wasn't expecting your support for an Arts Commission.

"You must have misunderstood me." Andrew corrected pleasantly

Barry continued explaining himself. "I thought we needed some more creativity in our public programs. We could have a film festival with movies like Wertmuller and maybe invite lecturers like Carl Sagan."

"I think he's dead." Andrew said.

Michael wasn't sure Barry had a grasp of the situation and steered the conversation back to the sculpture.

"No doubt the monument will have all the qualities of creative genius, whatever that is these days. Surely there's a maze of levels of permission to obtain. Some of it will be legal, but from my preliminary review of the deeds, most of it will be political. To be honest, in the best of all possible worlds, the county itself could actually purchase the parcels of land and dedicate them to support the monument. Even if the current owners were unwilling to sell, condemnation proceedings could be brought which would force the sale.

"I think the current owner is among the receivers of a bankrupt mining company." Andrew interjected.

Michael focused his attention on Barry. "To get to the point, assuming there's some perceived value in Alathon's proposed undertaking, is there any way you can help in the political arena?

Barry responded cautiously, "Without more information, it's hard to say if I will or won't support your client's enterprise. I don't know if I have the time.

Andrew was more enthusiastic. "I don't know anything about art and I'm unqualified to take the lead on a decision but I have a gut feeling that this deserves a hearing. Why don't you ask Beverly what she thinks?" He said to Barry.

Michael needed a lot of long-term help and he thought Andrew was pushing Barry too hard. He wanted him to back off a bit and give the guy room to make up his mind. He wondered who Beverly was and what she had to do with anything. "I think the best way to proceed," Michael said carefully, "would be to meet with Alathon, hear from him what he has in mind, and go from there. What if we kept your support in abeyance for the time being and simply schedule a meeting -- somewhere, sometime -- with our principals?"

Barry was not the kind of guy to admit that he didn't know what was going on and his ego was kicking back in. "I'd have to agree to that." He said confidently. "Stay in touch and let me know where and when we might meet. I'll break down to this extent; I'm generally in favor of the idea. But there are lots of pretenders to the throne out there. To get my support, I need to be sold on the project. But I'm open to salesmanship at this point."

"That's all I can ask for now." Michael said. "I'll get in touch with you as soon as I can locate Alathon. And Barry, there's an outside chance that we can participate in a leading edge of meaningfulness here."

"That's the main reason I'm donating my time and energy to this project." Andrew added.

Michael continued. "Perhaps after you've had an opportunity to place your stamp of approval on it, you'll get the same thrill."

"Perhaps." Barry responded.

Andrew rose from his chair to end the meeting. Michael

and Barry backed out the office.

Barry paused at the door and turned to Andrew. "I really did misunderstand. I'm looking forward to working with you."

Michael was at Darlene's desk leaving his phone number and calling Jim Bagnold, Harry Bain and Sam Cummings to contact him.

Hanging up the phone he said. "You've been a tremendous help and I'm in your debt. Thanks a lot Andrew."

"Not at all. Count me in on the next meeting."

Darlene watched Barry and Michael exit out onto the sidewalk. "What are those two up to?" She asked.

"They're just a couple of artistic geniuses who are going to teach us what meaningfulness is all about."

"It's about time." Darlene said.

Andrew's mind flew to Tony's bar and the hottest woman in town behind it. He thought what a fair and prosperous day this had been.

Barry and Michael walked up the sidewalk toward Michael's car.

"I want to be able to help with your project," Barry said, "I just need a better idea of what you're talking about.

At the car door Michael said. "What are you doing right now? Why don't we drive up to Eisenhower Tunnel?"

"I can't right now. How about next Wednesday." Barry replied.

■■■

When Philip and Theo arrived in Silverthorne, they were supposed to meet with a guy named Jake, who was referred to them by Lem. Jake was a camping guide who could possibly help them set up camp at Coon Hill. However, when they called him he let them know right away and very bluntly, that he didn't want to have anything to do with them. He did have the courtesy to refer him to his main competitor, Hugh. "Wonder who put the bur under his saddle?" said Theo surprised.

"Hang with Philip Alathon long enough and you'll get used to it."

When they met with Hugh, he said he was glad to help, but thought they were crazy to try to winter up there. Nevertheless, he knew of an old, deserted cabin that might possibly fit their needs. Hugh saddled up three horses, loaded two mules with some food and water, sleeping bags, axes, saws, and some narrow rope, and they began the ascent. They headed up Ptarmigan Pass Trail, then crossed over to Laskey Gulch Trail. En route they saw deer, elk, a mountain lion, and what had probably been a bear lair. The terrain was rough, but the trails passable. After about two hours in the saddle, Hugh pulled up, dismounted, and said they'd need to walk the next couple of hundred yards while he tried to locate the old cabin. He knew it was up here somewhere.

"Lead the way" Theo said and waited for Philip to grab his arm for guidance. "You missed lots of beautiful scenery and wildlife on the way up here." Philip just grunted and said "I'll stay here while you guys search." His mind was on the project.

Theo followed Hugh up a barely visible deer path for a few minutes when up ahead appeared what was left of an old log structure. Part of the tin roof was missing, the only two windows were uncovered, and the door was hanging on one hinge. The only thing inside was what appeared to be a makeshift stove of some sort, with the metal chimney still intact.

"With some work, I guess this could become livable," Hugh sighed, "but it'll still be colder'n the shady side of Siberia during a blizzard."

They walked back to where Philip was. He was sitting on a log, seemingly in a dream world. After telling Philip of their findings, Philip said "it's early November. The real blizzards don't come until January. Hugh, if you're willing – perhaps with some of your friend's help – to make the cabin habitable and stack lots stove wood up near enough to fetch, we'd be forever in your debt. We'd probably need to descend to civilization sometime in mid- to late-December while your horses can still make the trek. We have solar chargers for our cell phones, so we can stay in touch with you."

"And that forever debt can be discharged in immediate cold, hard cash." Hugh replied.

So the plan was laid. They stacked all the gear in the cabin, put some makeshift tarps over the window and fixed the door so it would shut.

Philip and Theo would spend the night, and Hugh would go back to Silverthorne with the animals, gather repair supplies and food, and return with help the next day.

Theo brought in enough firewood to last through the night, pulled a couple of short but large diameter logs inside for stools, got the stove lit and warmed up some dried soup for dinner. Finally Theo asked "OK, now we're here, what's next? We (or I) can see the tunnel by hiking just over that ridge behind us."

Taking his time to respond, Philip finally spoke. "What I need is for you to fully describe every single element of what's there. Tree types and sizes, all the flora and fauna, if any. The interstate, what the tunnel opening looks like. I'll hear the sound of the traffic and I'll smell the exhaust among the pine scents. I need to be able to see, sense, even feel, absolutely everything there is about this location so my mind's eye can grasp it all."

Theo understood. "But first we'd better get in touch with Michael." So he called Sharon, gave her their cell phone numbers, and got Michael's.

Michael called Theo asked if he and Philip could meet him at the tunnel Wednesday at, say, 11 a.m. Once they agreed, he called Barry to see if he could join them. Barry enthusiastically agreed.

****

On Wednesday, Michael and Barry pulled off into the parking lot off to the south of the tunnel. The wind was blowing at least 20 miles an hour, and here at almost 12,000 feet, it was chilly. It had been a gray day and Michael and Barry were dressed in the layers of clothing that were essential for comfort in the various temperatures of the highlands this time of year. Their heavier outer layers could be removed in the sunny lower elevations and replaced at the higher elevations or the shade. By adding a parka they could be comfortably exposed to the harsher elements. There was a map posted in the parking area which identified the tunnel's statistics: elevation, length, cross-section, ventilation, etc., etc. There was a rock-strewn, ragged peak about 1/4 mile northwest of the tunnel exit, identified on the map as Coon Hill. It was awesome against the bright-blue Colorado sky, almost seducing the onlooker with its ruggedness; a paradigm of what mountains were about.

A flurry of snow was falling, and Michael poured a last cup of coffee from the thermos he'd brought along and passed it to Barry. Michael was mostly unconsciously comparing this view to the view from his office in Manhattan. His id was super flabbergasted. He stood in sheer awe of this, his new surroundings.

"Christ." Michael said, "This is the top of the world." He'd impulsively brought Barry here to explain Philip's dream in more detail and was now trying to imagine how he was going to explain something he didn't know.

Michael thought he heard a sound in the distance behind him and when he turned he could see a couple of figures descending from up above the northern edge of the tunnel. The taller man was obviously following the lead of the shorter, and they appeared to be more intent on a conversation than on the narrow stream they were crossing. They continued down. Each would pause and gesture with varying degrees of force, then begin walking again down the deer trail leading to the base of the tunnel.

The scene brought fond memories back to Michael, recollections of hours upon hours of political, social and philosophical discussions from years ago. Although they were out of earshot, he could imagine the depth of their conversation. Finally, when they were within shouting distance, Michael yelled "Philip! T-Boy! Over here!"

Theo was slowing his pace to keep Philip near his shoulder. "Michael. God, it's good to see you again. How long's it been ... 2 ... 2 1/2 years ... can't remember? Anyway, how's things? Get settled yet? Have any trouble getting here?"

"What the hell you been doing up there." Michael shouted back.

Theo stepped adroitly down to the parking lot. Philip was a few short steps behind. "You know that Philip's reasons are often incomprehensible to us mere mortals."

Michael clasped Theo's hand. "It's great to be here." He said in greeting. "I'm getting a little cabin in Georgetown, and I'm ready to work. In fact I've already had some conversations with Art Wolltrip. Meet Barry Hollister, one of the Summit County Commissioners. Barry, meet Philip Alathon and Theo Boudreaux."

"Pleased to meet you. Michael, tell me more" Theo urged as he put his hand out blindly.

Michael had to be reminded of Philip's blindness and reached quickly for his hand. Feeling the warmth of his handshake, Michael remembered why they'd been such friends. Although they were diametrically opposed with respect to their chosen lifestyles, somehow, inexplicably, they were one with respect to values.

"Wolltrip is T-Boy's contact in the Breckenridge bureaucracy," Michael explained, "and Barry Hollister is a curious elected official who's right here."

Michael guided Philip's hand to Barry. "Good to meet you." Barry said, shaking Philip's hand awkwardly. "I came up here to get the story of your sculpture from Michael. Now I guess I'll get it from the source."

"There's a lot to talk about." Philip said.

"I assume I'm facing sort of northwest." Philip continued. "Where is the sun in relationship to that crag? At different times of the day -- at different sun, shadow, haze, and light combination it will change like a chameleon. The sounds of cars flying by, going in and out of the tunnel are a part of it. Even the smell of the vehicle fumes, rising up on the drafts of wind currents up the valley. See, Barry, over there where that 'no parking' sign is. That's roughly the location of the land parcel we're interested in."

Michael noted with amusement the surprise on Barry's face as he looked around for a sign that he couldn't locate but a blind man remembered from months or years ago.

"When you're coming out of the tunnel," Philip said, "that's the first thing your eyes focus on having been in the tunnel for an average of 47 seconds. That's the mean, the median is 56, and the mode is

40. Range from 36 to 72 seconds. Anyway, you've been driving, probably from Denver at least, and you've just sampled the beauty of Loveland Pass, and you're about to cross the continental divide ... ever give much thought to the continental divide, Barry?"

Without waiting for a response, Philip continued, "Phenomenal, utterly phenomenal. Glaciation, according to geologist's theories at least, caused this rift between east and west. And I really mean on a global scale. West is California, wedged uncomfortably between paradigmatic western democracy and dogmatic eastern liberalism; between New York, the center of this hemisphere, and Beijing, the center of the east. Beach bums and super-egos on the one hand, juxtaposed against peasants and primitivism, world leadership and poverty on the other. An abyss originated by glaciation!"

"And here we are, standing right on the apex of the division of the geological, if not the political world. You can almost feel the warmth of the moment creeping through your soles."

"And Man must make a statement here. And I am Man and I will make that statement, since no one else has cared to. That statement will be that these haunts of the gods, magnificent and sublimely remote as they are can be brought into dialog with the unlimited beauty that abides in Man's imagination. It's good and necessary".

"Every traveler blasting from that tunnel, like a slug from a shotgun barrel, will be placed in front of a mutually antagonistic presence of mind and mountain and have to acknowledge it. He'll have no choice. In his acknowledgement he will see Man 'as if for the first time'. He'll say 'truly it is so' and know that man alone is capable of creation. This project has to happen. It will edify Man as never before."

As Philip's grand vision echoed from the distant peaks Michael thought that they presented quite a curious assembly: a New York lawyer, a dilettante county official, an Avant garde artist and his poet aide. He thought this must be characteristic of the bizarre mix of talents that had to mesh to bring about work of public art. Barry was a little taken aback by Philip's diatribe, but he also recognized that Philip was quite a unique personality.

Philip caught his breath and turned instinctively in the direction of Michael. Why don't you come back up with us to the campsite, and we can talk along the way. It's about forty-five minutes from here...no, better make that an hour for a flat lander. Unless you're wearing your lawyer's uniform. T-Boy, does he have on his wingtips?"

"No. He looks like he just stepped out of a North Face catalog." Theo laughed.

"Well if you've got warm clothes there's a real mountain man back up at camp that I'm sure can produce a comfortable camp fire. Lock your car and let's climb.

Michael looked to Barry who shrugged in agreement and they began moving toward the path up to Coon Hill. Michael had hoped that Barry would be carried along by the force of Philip's personality and he was.

Philip listened intently as Michael tried to draw a verbal panorama, occasionally interrupting Michael with "how many degrees would you say" or "where is the sun in relationship to that crag"? Soon, they began the ascent back toward the campsite. All along the way, Michael and Theo kept offering Philip more elucidation of the scenery in his blurry sight with Barry trailing behind. Several pauses were necessary for Michael to catch his breath.

The elevation at the tunnel, where they would begin their ascent, was about 11,200 feet. They had to go over the ridge north of Coon Hill, which was about 12,800 feet, and then descend into the campground, on the other side of the ridge at about 11,000 feet. At the beginning of the trek, the ascent was gradual, but as they approached 12,300 feet, the incline became steeper and strewn with large rocks and boulders. At this elevation, climbing 500 vertical feet was like running a marathon. Breathing for Michael and Barry became more and more difficult, and they would walk a few steps, pause, breathe, walk some more, pause, and so on until they were at the precipice of the ridge. It had been about half an hour since they left the tunnel. At one of the pauses, Michael sat down on a boulder and just looked around. The continental divide over there to the east seemingly within walking distance, formed a barrier beyond which was the whole eastern part of the continent. This side of the divide was astounding; vast, hard and barren. He looked down upon the territory they had just traversed, and it was apparent that they had gained quite a bit of elevation. From this height, the stream at the bottom of the valley was barely more than a ribbon strung through the meadow, and the mountain ridges surrounded them and made him feel like he was in a bowl.

It was a little after three when they crossed the knoll up above the tunnel entrance and approached the camp, huffing and puffing. Although they had taken it fairly slowly, it was still a difficult climb. The view over the ridge from its precipice was the most stunning sight Michael had ever seen. There was a castle-shaped rock formation over to the left, and a beautiful, pine-studded valley below, with a trickle of a stream flowing through it. They stood there for a minute, just looking, then Theo and Philip headed off through some boulders. Finally, thank god, it was downhill to the cabin, only about 10 minutes away.

Michael couldn't help but notice the smell of something cooking over the camp-fire. Nostalgia again took over his thoughts momentarily as he recalled some unmatchable meals at places like Lodgepole, Spruce and Slumgullion Pass. The cook was introduced as Hugh, a six foot three redhead snatched right out of a Viking fiord and transported to the New World Nordic highlands of Colorado. Hugh had spent two days hauling up cabin repair materials, food supplies and cooking equipment, and cots. He repaired the cabin roof and door, and replaced the tarp on the windows with some heavy plastic.

Showing Barry and Michael around, Theo explained that Hugh had spent two days fixing up the cabin, and cutting stove and firewood.

Over the camp-fire, Michael rested against a log that he had drug with some considerable effort to the edge of the fire for just this purpose. Through the soft buzz of coffee and Southern Comfort the faces of Philip and T-Boy in the fire light could have been from half a lifetime ago.

From another corner of the fire and his own comfortable log Barry asked, "How long did it take you to get up here? And for that matter, Michael never explained why you're up here."

"To explain metaphor, you have to use it." Philip offered in reply but Barry didn't look satisfied with the answer.

Theo began telling the story of the trek up Ptarmigan trail.

"Coon Hill's elevation is about 12,400 feet." Theo began. "Hugh's plan was to head up the eastern fork of Ptarmigan trail. The trail splits about 3/4 mile out of Silverthorne. The west fork is a smoother traverse, but the east fork is shorter. We ascended about 1500 feet, then dropped off back down to where the west fork and east fork meet. The mules can easily handle the elevation. Hugh's only concern was whether Philip and I could handle it. After only about a mile and a half, he gained confidence in our wilderness abilities."

"Yea I asked them if they were going hunting." Hugh interjected from behind his bottle of Jack Daniels. "Hunting should be great up here this fall. We're not going there for hunting, they said. Blind men don't hunt. Well, I said, blind men don't usually pack either. I don't know what they do. Play harmonica maybe. But we're not hunting and we're not playing the harmonica so you tell me what they're doing? But I tell you being on the trail didn't seem to bother Philip here. His horse followed Theo's closely enough to stay out of danger."

"We'd been on the trail for about 3 hours." T-Boy continued. "Jake suggested we stop for lunch just on the lee-side of the first Williams Fork ridge. Some huge spruce trees formed a parasol between us and a royal blue sky. You should have seen it. There were enough dead trees and limbs to make a comfortable rest stop. The animals were holding up well but we needed to loosen the girths and let them rest. We had cheese sandwiches and dehydrated beans cooked over Hugh's SVEA stove. He talks like he's never heard of civilization but he's got all the comforts of home in his kit. Even at 9,800 feet, it lit fairly easily. The Swedes know about mountain gear!"

Hugh ignored the compliment. "My kit lets me live up here on my own terms. But these guys brought telephones, computers and who knows what else. They're climbing the Rocky Mountains to talk on the telephone!"

"We're here to improve things." Theo clarified. "We didn't rest for more than 1/2 an hour. Hugh wanted to make it up before dusk. The next mile or so was fairly level, and through some of the most beautifully pristine forest in all of Colorado. Gaining elevation at roughly a vertical mile an hour, the scenery was constantly changing. Sometimes, off to the left, the tip of some mountain would stand out and present a landscape which could only be committed to memory. I would have taken a photograph for you but pictures of mountains were inconsequential when compared to being among them. A photograph could only capture a few degrees of the perspective. There were no 'wide-angle lenses' that could envelop the moment of the scene. Then, off to the right would be the forest, deep dark chasms, wild fern, aged pine tree trunks, deep green foliage meeting brilliant blue skies so casually yet so forcefully that any human perspective only made the perceiver aware of his limitations.

"Toward the end of the forest, we headed up to Ptarmigan pass. We hadn't been on the trail for more than 20 minutes before my horse stopped abruptly, pointed its ears to the west, and in spite of my urging, simply refused to go any further. Hugh came alongside and panned the area. After rotating about 150 degrees his head stopped. Off to the southeast just out of range of easy sight was a brown bear and two cubs eating berries. The cubs could have cared less about the intrusion, but mom was upset to say the least. She stood up on her hind legs and let us intruders know in no uncertain terms that we were infringing on her territory. Her teeth were bared, saliva dripped from the corner of her mouth, and I thought her claws were to growing out this long."

Theo stretched his arms to their full extent.

"Assessing the situation," Theo continued. "Hugh rode right toward the bear. When he was within about 30 feet, he screamed at the top of his lungs -- yeigghehaamph. And the bear and her cubs scrambled off into the tundra, pissed off but safe. Hugh returned to where Philip and I were waiting and without a word, motioned us to continue up the trail. I had actually observed a Norse version of Davy Crockett. Geez."

"There's no point running from a bear." Hugh amplified. "And shitting in your pants doesn't help either. I can tell you that from experience. You may as well go straight at them and hope they fall for the bluff."

"I'm glad we had an impressionable bear." Philip commented.

Theo continued. "As we rode on, the shadows lengthened rapidly, and a chill began to set in. We emerged from the forest and in a blink, we were on the edge of tree line. Hugh yelled at us to stop, and we returned back to the edge of the forest. We were beside one of the unnamed tributaries to Laskey Gulch, a few hundred yards from the Grand/Summit County line, at about 11,200 feet.

"It was near dusk when we finally made it to the cabin, and the temperature began falling noticeably. Looking across the valley, a cloud of snow was barely discernible between us and the trees on the other side. Hugh got the mules unpacked, tied them up and fed them, and checked the hooves of all the animals. We had a quick dinner after getting the stove fired up, and all went to sleep. That's when we called Sharron.

"In the morning Hugh woke up early motioned us to come outside. A herd of elk was watering down near Laskey Gulch. Christ, there must have been 50 of the beautiful bovines, a couple with more than 12 points. We stopped and watched from atop our mounts, just stared at them -- probably much as the Utes had stared at herds of buffalo prior to the hunt a couple hundred years ago."

Hugh spoke up again. "Once you guys get settled in, you probably ought to go back down there and bag one of these cows. Should dress out at more than 200 pounds, enough to last you 'til spring."

"Those guys are better travelers than I thought." Hugh said. "I expected to be out at least two whole days. I asked them what their hurry was to get up to Coon Hill. Mr. Philip over there told me he just needed to come up and get a feel for the lay of the land. So, I told them it's none of my business, but why the fuck do you need to get the, as you say, 'lay of the land?' It's going to be fuckin' cold and windy up there this winter. Wind chills of 40 or more degrees below and they said, 'We know.' So I said, 'Got something to prove or what? 'scuse me. But christ, sane people try to avoid what you guys are headed into. Ever camped at this altitude in the winter before I asked? I mean, really even if the cold doesn't get you, the avalanches will. You guys had any avalanche training?' I asked. They said, 'No,' but they didn't seem too worried about it. To my knowledge, they could be mad men or criminals. But I had to make 'em let me be sure they're going to survive up here."

"Hugh's a yeoman." Philip interjected. "And as knowledgeable as he thinks he is."

Listening to T-Boy's stories, Michael was drifting on ocean waves of carefree nostalgia but the thought of the winter ahead pulled him back to shore and the business he was up here from New York to conduct. He related what he had learned so far, bringing Hollister into the picture and letting them know what he had learned about the deed, restrictions, easements, etc. He explained how it appeared that permission would be attainable but only with general public acceptance. A long-range plan would be required which took into account some sort of permanent endowment to cover future maintenance costs.

"It's my belief," Michael concluded, "that if Barry can be convinced to arouse the county's sensitivity to art in general, this could become a watershed project for the area."

Barry spoke up quickly. "I'm already convinced. In fact I'm astounded. Around this camp-fire are gathered some of the finest minds in the world, and I actually feel privileged. I just wish Beverly could be here to know the gravity of the moment. I have no doubt that I'll return to my role as county commissioner and champion this project. I don't have a choice. The main question is do I have the clout? I'm the new kid on the block, and the other commissioners are ingrained into a mediocre maintenance of the status quo."

"I think you'll need to get their attention." Theo suggested. "Philip has always been good at that. But I know that you'll need a gimmick, a platform from which to sell the project. You'll have to think of something that works locally."

"We could start right here." Barry said with confidence. He was clearly anxious to do his part for the team. "Maybe Hugh can tell us what the common citizen would think of a new work of art celebrating these glorious mountains."

"These mountains are already full of garbage." Hugh said abruptly, "The continents are filling up with their garbage. The stench rises up to here. A million years of technology to learn how to make shit flow uphill."

Only at that moment did Michael realize how drunk Hugh had become. He sensed danger, "Some of it's getting cleaned up." Theo said without provocation, "We can hope for a better future." then changed the subject, "But for now, Barry and I need to get back down the mountain while there's still enough light." Then they left saying "We'll stay in touch."

Hugh took another swallow of whiskey. It looked like half a fifth went down his throat.

In the morning as Theo left the cabin to take a piss, Hugh was checking the shoes of the mules and getting into his backpack. Surrounded by the black and gray of his parka, Hugh's blue eyes, shining with hangover, appeared almost transparent.

"I guess you're leaving?" Theo stated the obvious.

"Well, yes. I'm going back to Silverthorne like we talked about yesterday. Let me know if I can do anything else to help"

"But after what you said last night."

Hugh looked away. "I don't know what I said last night." He turned to go. "I'll be in touch."

With a practiced slap on the rump of his lead mule began the pack train moving away from the edge of the camp and back down toward Hamilton Gulch. He paused—hesitated for a moment and looked back over his shoulder. "They're not going to let you build that statue."

"Who isn't?"

"Lem told you."

"When did you talk to Lem?"

"Lem talked to Jake and Jake told me. I've said all I'm going to say. I've said too much."

Chapter Eight

"....Being's poem, just begun, is man." - Heidegger

****

As fall gave way to winter at Coon Hill it was now cold most of the time. When Theo first rolled out of his sleeping bag in the morning, frost, or a new dusting of snow, covered everything outside the cabin. He would throw a few pieces of kindling on the smoldering remains of last night's fire in the old, make-shift stove. Their coffee pot, left over from last night's conversation, needed only some melted snow to get perking again. The only problem here was that for every handful of snow, only a quarter inch of water would result. As Theo kept shoveling handfuls of snow into the coffee pot, Philip began to rouse. Wafting through the air, the smell of coffee would prepare them for yet another day -- a day which would require more wood to be cut for the stove, more snow to be collected for the water bag, and more thoughts to be directed toward why they were there in the first place.

They took daily walks to various observation points near the tunnel where Theo described what he was seeing in great detail. In time Philip could have made it most of the way alone. Where there had never been a trail before, they had beaten enough of a path that the way could be felt easily under foot-- except on those mornings after a dusting of snow. The various destinations required different degrees of dexterity to reach. Philip insisted on covering all the ground even if that meant Theo had to lead him over 100 yards of boulders rolled there by centuries of avalanches. Theo suggested that the precariousness of the trek might prove as fruitful to Philip's imagination as the arrival. "All-too Hegelian" Philip said. "We're not involved in process, but in accomplishment. We'll build and the construction will be a fixed place and dwelling of thought. Dwelling is the manner in which mortals are on the earth."

Theo would just nod, unnoticed to Philip, and they would continue wending their way across the boulders. Sometimes, Philip would stop because he could hear the echo of water trickling downward beneath 20-30 feet of boulders. In another few thousand years, this avalanche chute could become a river, and the mountain could be split in half.

Finally, they would get to a point where the portals to the Eisenhower Tunnel were in view as they pierced the continental divide. Driving through the tunnel, and exiting the western portal, Coon Hill jutted immediately up to the north. Then, after continuing only a few hundred feet out of the tunnel, the Ten Mile Range came into view around behind Coon Hill.

It was exactly 637 feet out of the tunnel, where Philip decided the sculpture should be placed, and it was the Ten Mile range, beyond Coon Hill, that would form the backdrop for his piece. Coon Hill served, from this perspective, only to define the right-most curtain of the stage.

As a driver went by to the south of the sculpture, Coon Hill would come into the picture, but only in sort of retrospect. The sculpture would be designed with the frame of a rear view mirror in mind. It had to be built so that the passers-by would have an aesthetic experience even as they drove past the sculpture, whether they stopped to look at it or not. The sculpture had to speak to a kinetic audience but against expectations. It would be such that no matter from what angle it was viewed, it would appear the same. Philip's sculpture would be, in Heideggerian terms a site for the disclosure of Being to man, albeit sometimes transient. And the piece would need no other justification.

Upon leaving the tunnel the top of Peak Two of the Ten Mile range was at an angle of about five degrees above the observer's horizontal sight line. To be significant, the top of the sculpture needed to be exactly 2 degrees above that. Philip's geometry wasn't capable of determining the actual size of the sculpture, but Theo, calculator in hand and a knowledge of trigonometry remaining in his brain from the days before he was a poet, made the calculations. So the sculpture had to be about 77 feet tall.

Philip began to give shape to his internal vision. To realize Dancing Star as Cheri, several sensual perceptions had to be merged in the sculpture. Using the words of ballet, the 'port de bras' (carriage of the arms) had to be 'courrone', and the movement of the body had to be the middle step of a 'grand jete en tournant' or 'jete entrelace'. These forms would intimate man's freedom. And these kinetic concepts would have to be wrapped up in a static sculpture which twisted and pointed to itself as the magnificence of man in-and-among the sublimity of nature's most magnificent mountains.

He would gesture with his arms encircled above and around his head trying to emulate the 'port de bras' -- his hands, palms inward, formed a continuous curve with the forearm. His fingers would be grouped freely but softly in their joints, thumb barely touching the middle finger, unbent wrist.

It was quite a strange sight, Philip moving around, gesturing, circling, spinning, with hiking boots and heavy parka, his large hands trying to define how the monument to man among the mountains must be. Theo didn't say much other than for Philip to watch out lest he trip over a rock and fall off the side of the mountain.

Around the camp-fire conversation about art became more tangible. Michael was in Colorado often enough to have acquired the heart and lungs of a local. The hike up to Coon Hill had become just like a walk to the corner for a newspaper. He joined Philip and Theo for regular reports on the real estate angle of the project and excursions into speculation about its meaning.

"Dancing Star will be viewed coming and going..." Philip said. "...striking astonishment to viewers opening into the clearing as they came out of the tunnel. Eyes will be drawn to her. Neck muscles, straining as heads turned to the right following Dancing Star would finally give up. She will be where they just couldn't not notice her. She will command the space. For many, she will flicker past windows of air-conditioned cars headed to mountain vacations without stopping to admire and participate in her glory. Those who decided to park in the nearby parking area and view her up close, the detail would fill them with awe. For some, she will brand memories, indelibly."

"Aren't a lot of people going to miss the significance?" Michael pondered.

"This is The Continental Divide -- not just some piddly ridge line." Philip elaborated. "Anything here is lifted to the significance of the timeless Earth. Dancing Star, claiming her space as hers alone will bestow, even ordain her presence. She will challenge passers-by to acknowledge her relationship to the universe."

"And if they don't?" Michael insisted.

"Dancing Star will remain confident of her place, her circumstance, her whimsy, her belonging-here. She will occupy what formerly had been only emptiness, but she will command the space where she is with pride."

"I usually don't think of the space between me and a grand view as empty."

"I agree. I should choose my language more carefully. What she will replace isn't emptiness but nothingness. She'll fill a new space with being. Suddenly, where there is nothing, she will -- magnificently -- reveal being and fill her environment with meaning. She will both belong there as if grow from the rock and in the same moment be an odd invention. She will represent man's genius, clumsily bashed against nature while she stands there as part of its domain."

"Hasn't the spirit of the modern age been man's conquest of nature? I'm not sure that's turned out all that well."

Theo spoke up unexpectedly. "The spirit of this age isn't contained in art. Artists have known that intuitively. They have been "anti-artists" for a hundred years."

"If artists are not making art..." Michael asked. "...if they're not concerned with what's good, beautiful or true who is?"

Theo replied. "Photographers, reporters, movie producers, ad agencies, architects, industrial designers-they create beautiful or meaningful work every day. They have the capacity to show people at their best. They can uphold ideals of justice or love. They can give pleasure and comfort and make life bearable. Isn't that what art is?"

Philip answered him. "Art shouldn't be something that puts people to sleep."

"So Nietzsche was wrong?" Theo knew that putting Philip at odds with Nietzsche would give him pause. "Does affirmation of life lead to consolation and sleep?"

"Life and status quo are not the same thing. Art shouldn't make people stupid and stimulate them to buy stuff they don't want."

"Art doesn't choose the time in which it's made."

"Artists have to choose. They have to turn and be open to what's being concealed in time."

Michael offered a different explanation. "I think artists just aren't capable anymore. They couldn't make anything if they wanted to. Present company excepted of course. Artists have lost the skills to respond to their age on the level of work?"

"That's pretty good Marxist thought." Theo concluded. "...coming from someone who makes a living liquidating businesses and pension fund investments so that Wall Street spiders can suck the life out of them. Or is bloodsucking what we call work in America these days."

Michael was reminded of Theo's outbursts from years ago and wasn't offended. "Even an idealist has gotta eat."

Philip turned the conversation back to his own immediate concerns. "I know and understood the spirit of Dancing Star now. The dimensions are established. Whirling, spiraling, 77 feet tall, "port de bras" and all. Her face is still an enigma. Like you said Michael, how is she of this world. Does she look down on the traffic with the benign countenance of a representative of the chamber of commerce welcoming the tourists to spend their money in style or would she be an aloof mountain goddess, eternal and indifferent."

"What view of the nature of understanding does the possibility of metaphor presuppose?" Theo encouraged.

"She will be beautiful but not Cheri's cosmopolitan vogue. She has to have a face as clear and pure as the mountains that surround her. I know I can work that out. Some harder questions, however, remain. What materials to use and how to get her constructed."

Michael added. "All along assuming that permission will be granted and funding available."

"That's the part of the process that I like least."

"Like any artist, I'm challenged to make my ideals work in the real world like they do in my imagination. This is no small task. It would be great if the piece would come together merely as a matter of my willing it. Unfortunately, there's more to it than imagination."

"But that would strip the work of time and matter." Theo insisted. "Fortunately, there is more to it than imagination. There is the thing itself."

"Philip has to be artist, architect and engineer." Michael was trying to be helpful. "As artist, he will be comprehensive -- creating Dancing Star's concept and fitting her into her environment. As architect, he will arrange her material around a coherent plan and supervise her production. As engineer, he will make sure she will be sturdy, and able to withstand time, nature and the elements -- pitfalls frolicking god's place in the paths of mortals."

Philip continued. "Much of my work in the past has been intended to disintegrate over time, to recognize the bond between life and death in nature and to defer to the power of the elements. Dancing Star will resist time. She will be designed for high wind loads and "mild" earthquakes. Local conditions will require other considerations and increase structural requirements. The traffic along I-70 creates vibrations that can slowly but surely cause deterioration in some media. Some 5 million vehicles a year pass through the tunnel. At least ten percent of them, are 18-wheelers. This is relevant, and continual vibrations can't be ignored. The sculptural material has to speak authoritatively -- it has to represent an idea in such a way that its right to be is unquestionable. It also has to meet strength requirements. What would the material be?"

"The mountains are rock and trees." Theo said plainly. "Dancing Star has to either blend with those materials by using them, or she has to be obstinately rebellious."

"Stainless steel, bronze, and cement are as out of place in the mountains as marshmallows are in fishing streams."

Michael offered. "How could she maintain her presence, her assertiveness, and still fit in?"

"She will draw attention to herself by conformity or by difference. By blending or by antithesis." Philip continued. "A lot of things have to be considered regarding the actual execution of Dancing Star. Because of the necessary fluidity of the dancer, her curves have to be ... just that, really curves."

"Her size would seem to eliminate carving, if marble or granite is what you have in mind." Michael responded. "77 feet is just too big a piece of rock. The need for perpetual maintenance, would seem to preclude wood."

"You're right. We don't want her painted -- that's for sure. Paint is a pain in the ass when put in the perspective of perpetuity. It would require too much maintenance. No, she needs to be able to withstand time just as these mountains have."

"So what does that leave you?"

"I have subconsciously been envisioning bronze all along, for its elasticity. A 77 foot sculpture could be cast in several pieces and hauled to the tunnel."

"Have you been working in bronze?" Michael asked.

"I understand the rudiments of bronze mold building from some preliminary work I did with the owner of a foundry in Casper, Wyoming. My proposal for the museum in Fort Wayne, Indiana fell through but I learned that even though the process of casting wall plaques and busts of community leaders is much the same as the creation of the Statue of Liberty. I couldn't trust the work to anyone who didn't have extensive experience with monumental bronzes."

Theo added. "The natural alternative is cement which would be another specialized technical challenge."

Philip continued. "Once erected, Bronze would be relatively problem free. It's more pliable than concrete, and therefore able to withstand more natural shocks. A 77 foot bronze would have to be cast in at least two pieces. Four or Five would be better. But the union of the pieces would be a smooth weld, and virtually unnoticeable. Precast reinforced concrete is durable and reasonably cost effective. However, it could be difficult to get a choice of colors in concrete. The usual possibilities are gray, white, buff, or warm tone. Concrete also typically varies in color from batch to batch and that might cause a problem   especially since we've already discarded the painting option. Making a smooth match where the parts join could also abrogate color continuity and lead to future maintenance problems with the joints. But ultimately, concrete just can't withstand the vibration."

Theo concluded. "Much of this is just for your information, Michael. Philip has become convinced that Dancing Star will have to be realized in bronze."

Philip agreed. "It was as much intuition as reason. The stuff I'm shaping is really space anyway. The details of the material substance will have to fall into place later. To bridge the distance that separates the viewer from the viewed the space the sculpture occupies has to impress the viewer just as much as what was viewed. In this setting, space is the primordial element. These are the mountains for Christ's sake, and space, when you're in the mountains, is not something you can easily ignore. A 14,000 foot peak is so awesomely noticeable that even from a distance of thirty miles, it seems like you could reach out and touch it." "I remember my first trip to the Grand Canyon." Theo added. "From the canyon rim the raging Colorado river appeared to be no more than a slender thread, meandering harmlessly below. The same perspective had apparently been that of the Indians who first stumbled onto that magnificent wonder. Thinking they could more or less saunter down to an innocuous stream for water, they soon learned that it took the better part of a day to make the trek down and back. An illusion. The surging river's forces at the bottom of the canyon were capable of killing people. Distances, among the haunts of the gods, are deceiving. Everything, from god's-eye-view, becomes beautiful and benign. It is only on the human scale that God's creations are murderous."

Philip looked up from the fire and pointed toward the divide. "Do you see something moving just below the ridge line?"

Startled by the urgency of Philips question, Theo and Michael snapped their heads in the direction of the ridge.

"Not really." Michael said.

"It could have been someone in a white robe." Theo observed. "But that's not likely."

At the same moment Theo and Michael realized that they were commenting on something seen by a blind man. Philip had become so comfortable with his blindness that they had forgotten his affliction.

"It's true." Philip answered their querying looks. "I thought I was beginning to perceive more bits of light through these eyes. I didn't say anything, because I've been living in such a world of imagination that I wasn't sure."

"I thought our trips over to the tunnel had become easier each day." Theo was taking the good news in stride. "I thought it was because your intuitions had become so fine-tuned but it was because you were seeing more with each trip."

"What had formerly been darkness," Philip said, "became dark tree trunks. What formerly had been artistic vision became blurred light. I was dubious about whether my imagination was perceptive or whether my perceptions were imaginative. I just didn't know. But I've felt for a while that we were not alone in camp and I think I've seen that white figure watching us from a distance more than once."

"He's the one blowing the trumpet." Theo laughed.

"Would you explain that in a little more detail?" Michael interjected.

"We've heard a trumpet blast from the distance." Theo explained.

"So somebody is sneaking around your camp?" Michael asked with some concern. "This isn't funny."

Philip replied. "We've heard voices, noises and flashes like an explosion. We thought it might be a mild earthquake. There's nothing to be concerned about. We're not on the moon up here. There might be other people around and things going on that we don't know about."

"Some unusual things have happened." Theo allowed. "Some of our canned vegetables were missing and I found them buried in the fire. I just thought we'd dropped them. With a blind man keeping stock things get misplaced. And by the way, Philip, I'm glad to know your eyesight is returning. Thanks for getting around to reassuring me."

Philip smiled his enigmatic smile and continued the story. "A rock came loose from up above and crashed into part of our store of water, then the next morning our drinking water had turned sour."

"That was the morning after the strange light in the sky nearly overhead. We never could explain that."

"And a trumpet?" Michael asked.

"Possibly. I think we did hear a trumpet."

"Probably an elk. If it's sabotage," Michael realized. "It could be Hugh. He left here pretty pissed about your plans to mess up his mountains with some of your modern art. Maybe he's hanging around out here and screwing things up."

"Not everything is screwed up." Philip said. "Only a part of the camp was in the path of the rock and only about a third of the water was sour. If that's Hugh up there, he can do whatever he wants to us and we couldn't stop him. He could make us and this whole camp disappear and no one would ever find us."

Theo added. "Philip's right. It doesn't add up to sabotage. It doesn't add up at all. It's just a set of coincidences. Or maybe Philip's elevated state of consciousness is focusing cosmological purposes on Coon Hill."

"I still think you should be careful." Michael said and he looked back toward the continental divide to see if anyone else was creeping around out there in a white robe.

"Before the blizzards begin, we probably need to think about heading down mountain for the remainder of the winter," Philip announced. "Better give ol' Hugh a call and see if he's still willing."

A call from Felicity reminded Michael that Thanksgiving was only three days away, so he made reservations on Delta. Nearly six hours to Hartford, including a layover in Detroit.

On the drive to Denver, Michael had mixed emotions. On the one hand, he was anxious and excited to see his family. On the other, he had begun to enjoy his work, his acquaintances, his surroundings and his life in the mountains. "Oh, well," he thought, "let the chips fall where they may."

Felicity met him at the airport, and when Michael saw her, some of the mixing of his emotions were allayed. God, was she a sight for sore eyes! They hugged and kissed and Fel said "The kids can't wait to see you and my parents are eager to have you explain why you've deserted us for this hiatus in Colorado. Driving to her parent's house, Michael brought her up to date on the project. She seemed interested and even mentioned that her mother, Elsa, might be of some help. But her primary concern was their relationship and his relationship with their kids.

Upon arrival at the Hollister 'estate', the kids ran out and nearly knocked Michael over as they jumped into his arms. "When are you coming back home?" Michelle asked. "Do you have any presents for us?"

Fortunately, when Michael was in the Denver airport, he remembered to get them something. Bronco stuffed animals, Colorado coloring books, a picture book of mountains, mining camps. Wild flowers and elk, deer, bears, foxes and wildcats. They seem to like their gifts, but continued to hang on to Michael. He couldn't help but be overwhelmed by their love. Fel watched approvingly but cautious. She didn't know when he would be back permanently. Elsa and Nelson came out and gave him big hugs, and Michael felt, strangely, at home.

Inside, with the kids in his lap and a gin-and tonic in his hand, Michael brought them up to date on what he was doing. Elsa seemed unusually interested in the project and even mentioned that he should keep her informed about it because she might be of some help. After a light dinner of mostly appetizers, Michael admitted his tiredness, and they all retired. In their bedroom, after the kids had played and snuggled, Felicity sent them to their bedrooms. Recognizing Michael's state of being, she slipped under the cover with him and uttered simply "Honey, I love you more than you'll ever know."

The next day, Thanksgiving, the adults enjoyed some mid-morning Mimosas as Elsa kept watch over the help as they prepared the feast, Michael and Felicity strolled over the perfectly manicured grounds. Fel felt like she wasn't making the normal connection with Michael, so she asked "What's on your mind?"

At that point Michael responded, "You know, when I took on this 'assignment', I knew it could be transformative. And Fel, it has been, but not for the reasons you might expect. I've actually been caught up in Philip's, I don't know, 'magic'. He's an incredible human being. He can turn everyday experience into a thought-provoking series of contemplation. It's as if he has an understanding of things that are so far removed from the ordinary, that one feels overwhelmed in his presence. Those days, years ago, when we camped together in Wyoming, it seemed to me to be more Southern Comfort than anything else. But in retrospect, I realize how brilliant Philip was. Way ahead of his time."

They enjoyed a glorious meal, unfortunately keeping the conversation rather banal while entertaining the kids. After eating, Nelson and Michael went into the study for a cigar and cognac. Nelson had finally accepted Michael as more than a hick from Texas when Michael's prestige in New York began to blossom.

"I want you to know that even though I have no understanding of what you're trying to accomplish, I'm behind you one hundred percent."

****

When he returned from Connecticut, Michael scheduled a meeting with Harry Bain, the Summit County Land Use director, and Sam Cummins in charge of inter-governmental relations.

After explaining his purpose, Michael asked them if they could play a role in helping with the project. Both said they would speak with their counterparts at the state level. What they did know was that the land in question was owned by a foreign firm represented by a firm in Seattle called Chance-Spell. Interstate 70 was on a State-owned easement across the property.

Michael called Chance-Spell, and was given the phone number for a person named Darcy Rios-Doria. He called that number, introduced himself and was about to explain the reason for his call, when the very pleasant voice on the other end said simply "I've been wondering when you'd call." A bit taken aback Michael barely uttered "Huh." Darcy went on to explain that she became aware of interest in the property through Andrew Wolltrip's office (she didn't reveal how she became aware!), and suggested that, since she was already in Breckenridge, perhaps they could meet. Still a bit surprised by this recent turn of events, Michael only said "Sure. How about tomorrow, say 10 a.m. at the County Commons – and I'd like to bring along another interested party." She agreed.

Michael met Barry at The Prospector for coffee before heading over to the County Commons. When Barry learned that they were meeting Darcy, he, too, was surprised. What could a bartendress have to do with that property?

When they arrived at the County Commons, Darcy was already there, waiting for them just outside the library. Michael whispered to Barry "Geez, I wasn't expecting that."

"Nor, I."

"How nice to meet you" Darcy began. "Who's who?"

"I'm Michael Lovell" he said extending his hand "and this is Barry Hollister, Summit County Commissioner and potential aide to what we're trying to accomplish up on I-70, just west of the tunnel."

"I'm honored Barry. Who's we? And what are you trying to accomplish?" she asked, shaking Barry's hand.

"Let's find a spare room inside where we can get comfortable and try to bring you up to speed." As they walked inside Michael continued "We'd like to know what your connection to that parcel of land is, too."

I represent foreign clients who own the parcel, and they will pretty much do with it what I recommend.

After they told Darcy what they had in mind and described the project, Darcy finally offered "OK, I believe that Philip's project has merit, and I'm willing to see if my clients would consider it. They probably will, since much of what I've suggested over the years has turned out well for them-- not necessarily about this parcel but their other interests in the US. I will suggest a renewable, 50 year lease as long as they remain in control of the mineral rights. Suggest also that we keep this under the covers for the time being.

Michael's beliefs about why anyone would have an interest in that parcel were confirmed. He assumed there must be uranium, or some similar valuable resource up there. He also briefly considered what 'under the covers' might be like with this luscious businesswoman.

"We couldn't ask for more" Barry added, thinking wait 'til Beverly hears about this.

Michael kept up a day by day communication with Barry. Barry couldn't help with the research into the property, which had turned out to be less complex than Michael had anticipated, but Michael wanted to be sure that Barry was making progress on the political front or at least not screwing anything up.

Barry had invited Michael to the wedding of a Hollister family friend. The announcement read "You are cordially invited to ski-in to our wedding at the Peak 9 Warming House". Barry's close family, led by the estimable Nelson Hollister was in town for the event.

The Colorado resorts compete to open the ski season. The first to open gets a premium in publicity in the newspapers. The fiercest rivalry is between Keystone and Loveland. Keystone had opened two weeks earlier but Loveland was open by Halloween and Michael skied out into a perfectly clear November afternoon with fresh light powder under his skis and dry invigorating mountain air filling his lungs.

The wedding party met at the quad chair-lift and rode it to the top of the mountain. When the happy couple got off the lift, the party had formed an arcade of ski-poles for them to ski under on the way to the warming house. Once there, to music provided by a local country and western band, they skied up to an archway constructed of snow, recited a brief wedding oath, and were married by a Summit County Justice of the Peace who was also a member of the ski-patrol. Some 30 cases of champagne and 150 pounds of hors d'oeuvres were served not only to the wedding party, but to anyone who happened to ski by. The wedding party skied as a group for a couple of hours, then the newlyweds slipped off in their Range Rover to honeymoon in a mountain retreat leaving the rest of the guests and party crashers to finish the champagne.

Michael mixed in with the other guests and watched over the celebration looking for an opportunity to meet Barry's family. The wedding party had an unmistakable aura of old New Haven charm. Michael, being a virile, albeit virtuous young man torn by time and circumstance from his wife's bed, was more than commonly attentive to the nuances of female pulchritude. From his first introduction into Felicity's society he had remarked how the right bearing, style, gesture and attention to the detail of fashion could create the impression of great beauty in a women who's actual physical endowments were quite plain if not actually doggy. Self-confident poise born of privilege and educational opportunities might create the impression that rich women are more beautiful than the ordinary kind.

Michael was suddenly brought up short by a vision of perfection whose integration of element and design absolutely defied analysis. He was fascinated. Swaying gently at the front of the room and watching the band was a tall, lean, red headed women with the grace of a classical dancer, the deftness of a bullfighter, the self-confident poise of a cornerback and the beauty of a - wait a minute - barmaid he'd seen working at Tony's. But it couldn't be - what's her name? - Darcy. Darcy the barmaid was in every detail, for lack of a better word, a blue-ribbon slut. This woman was obviously the daughter, colleague, wife, or date of one of the country's most well-heeled gentlemen. But it was Darcy or her identical cousin. Somehow she seemed slimmer and taller. Her breasts and hands were smaller. Her lips were tighter and her eyes larger. Her feet probably smelled better. Michael was doubly fascinated.

Darcy crossed the room and joined several of the other women from Connecticut around Nelson

Hollister. Even the mothers and fathers of the bride and groom appeared deferential to the Hollisters. The Hollister patriarch and matriarch displayed an understated elegance which Michael noted in contrast to the more forward manner of Felicity's equally wealthy and socially connected family. Barry danced with his mother and then with his sister. The sister had obviously married well and her husband moved within the family with the total confidence of an heir.

Then in the midst of all of this high tone there was Beverly. She laughed out loud. She kissed Barry spontaneously and innocently. She sat on the stage and flirted with the band. She danced by herself if no-one else was dancing. Michael wondered if Mr. and Mrs. Nelson Hollister had any private thoughts about Barry's ski-bum-bimbo.

As if reading Michael's thoughts Barry appeared at his shoulder with two glasses of champagne. "Beverly seduced Dianne and Nelson as easily as she seduced me." Barry explained.

Michael accepted a glass of champagne and assumed Diane to be Mrs. Hollister.

"She really is as innocent as she is beautiful." Barry observed. "Look at her hugging the Grand Dame over there without a thought of class or propriety. Beverly's naïveté is real. Her family had few enmities, and the ones they had apparently didn't rub off on her. She dances through life oblivious to anger."

"Does your family know how serious you are about her?" Michael noted to himself that he wouldn't have asked that question if he wasn't coming to think of Barry as a close friend.

"As much as I regret the thought of it, I really do care what my parents think." Barry replied. "As I've spent more and more time with Beverly, I've come to respect her in a way I'd not originally thought possible. As you know we're a very well educated and connected family. Beverly has little formal education and no interest at all in world affairs but she's wise. She understands things with a simple question or gesture that cuts through a lot of bull shit."

"I myself have noticed a marked absence of bull shit in Beverly." Michael added.

"I thought my mother could see that too. I took Nelson off fishing and left Beverly and Dianne to fend for themselves. Dianne and my sister invited Beverly to join them for tea. I guess it was a test like 'Pygmalion'. For all I know Beverly might have held forth all afternoon about the pleasures of slopping the hogs back in Tennessee but somehow it all came out in her favor. Dianne really seems to be able to love

Beverly against her better judgment. And you know what Beverly said about Dianne?"

"She said your mom would make a good hog slopper?" Michael offered. "If the flash of her diamonds didn't scare the old boar."

"She told me, 'Your mother is very obliging'. That's Dianne exactly. My mother's life is ruled by duty. And in the end Beverly knows our relationship to Dianne will be in terms of duty. We are a very business-like family. We keep things to ourselves -- not so much out of necessity as out of tradition."

Nelson Hollister was making his way past some inebriated dancers and approaching Barry and Michael. Barry took the champagne glass from Michael. "Father I'd like you to meet Michael Lovell."

"Yes. Barry's been telling me about your work together." Nelson said, with a firm shake of Michael's hand. "I thought a county commissioner's job was mostly filling potholes but Barry's telling me Philip Alathon's next magnum opus is coming to the Continental Divide."

Michael had gone over in his mind how he might gracefully broach the subject of Philip's project in the presence of Barry's father and here was the man himself jumping right into it. "I'm doing what I can." Michael said. "But this business is turning me into more of a land agent than I wanted to be. Your son has been very helpful."

"Land is not my forte." Nelson said. "But I've been talking to Barry a little bit about art. I've been benefactor to a few social projects in the past and I try to stay up with art scene, such as it is these days. Do you remember the "Nothing Players" troupe in Hartford from a while back or the"Proto-Symbolists" in New York? I was attracted to popular avant-garde movements (if that's not a contradiction) which met only two criteria: intelligibility and improvisation. Alathon's always been a shade too harebrained for me but I'm following Barry's confidence in this thing and trusting that he's not about to go off the deep end without a good look at it."

"I was talking to Philip this morning." Michael risked interrupting. "I think that what he has in mind will be much more obliging than what you've seen in the past."

Nelson continued. "Now really isn't the time to talk about this but I wanted to meet you before we fly back to Connecticut tonight. When you've got the land and construction funding in place I can walk you through the details of an arts maintenance trust and its tax ramifications for investors. You'll want to set up an endowment of at least two million dollars with about twenty percent invested and added to the principal in perpetuity to ward off inflationary pressures."

Mr. Hollister was obviously enjoying the prospect of taking part in a new venture while cautiously delaying his participation until after substantial risk was taken by other earlier investors. Michael decided to take a chance on pressing the issue a little further. "If we could get some informal indication of your interest that might help us to raise the construction money. I'll be visiting my family back in New York. Do you know Elsa Horowitz?"

Nelson's eyes widened in surprise. "Of course I know Elsa Horowitz. By reputation mostly."

"Elsa is my wife's mother." Michael explained.

"Our interests have converged on several cultural affairs issues." Nelson said. "Somehow I've never met her socially."

What Nelson meant was that the New York Jewish establishment and the East Coast Mayflower aristocracy were interwoven in the financial life of the city but that they did not typically socialize. Michael finished his thought. "Perhaps in the near future we can get together for a strategy session."

"That would be interesting." Nelson said. "Keep me informed."

The lights in the hall began to dim. Most of the wedding party were already returning to their condos for the evening. The champagne supply had run dry and that had directed the locals to the exits. Nelson excused himself and joined his wife to search for their parkas and gloves. Michael had never tried to get Felicity's mother directly involved in one of his enterprises. He often suspected that she had pulled strings when she could but this would mean asking her to get involved back in her own world where there were long standing rules and boundaries that he barely knew existed. Michael hoped that he had not pushed too hard too soon.

The Hollisters turned back at the door to wave goodbye to Michael. They paused and Michael watched as Darcy Rios-Doria hurried on tip toes to the door to catch up with them. Darcy also looked back across the room to Michael and smiled. She held Nelson's arm as they left.

Michael called Theo with the encouraging news. "I had the distinct impression that Nelson Hollister was ready to put some real money into the enterprise." Michael told Theo. "He actually mentioned two million dollars without any prompting from me. Our Barry Hollister connection may actually turn out to be the key to the whole thing."

Chapter Nine

"What is this great thing that men compel themselves to seek?

****

At Friday's meeting of the county Commissioners, Barry had persuaded them to get behind the idea of a sculpture at the tunnel. Unwilling to make the possibly controversial project decision themselves, they agreed to present it to the voters as a referendum. Barry thought "At least some progress anyway." The referendum was announced in Saturday's and Sunday's papers.

Ullr-fest was an esoteric celebration dedicated to a mostly unheralded Norse god of archery and snow but it had become one of the most important winter events in Breckenridge. In mid-January, there were parades, fireworks, the queen's ball, drunkenness and generally a bacchanalian revelry associated with (or giving an excuse for) a giant party. Ullr is pronounced just as it's spelled, uuh-ler. Regular guests to the ski-area made reservations six to nine months in advance for the occasion which was as close to Mardi Gras as you get in the mountains.

In Late December, Willie Meinstrom had determined that his store, Herr Meinstrom's, would be a participant in the festivities. Willie's ego wouldn't let him do less than enter the best float in the Ullr parade. A businessman at heart, a sexist in spirit, Willie surmised that the float should be big and adorned with beauty. Of course, Beverly immediately came to mind.

After returning from the meeting with Michael and Darcy, Barry brought Beverly up to speed on the sculpture project.

On Monday Beverly returned to work at Meinstrom's charged with the intention of turning Willie's float into publicity for the Department of Art Domains and Philip's sculpture. Once the store was open and the counter displays reorganized for the new week she returned to the subject of the float.

"Willie," Beverly said. "I agreed to play the hot babe shaking her fanny on your float this year but I want to do that under certain conditions --mainly, that the float have some social significance."

"You know that float's going to represent the business. I wouldn't want to do anything distracting. What do you mean by social significance?"

"Only that we should make a statement in our float that could help make a difference."

"Did that answer my question?"

"Yeah. Look Willie. We're both human beings on this planet just like our employees and our customers and all the skiers and even the ski-bums in town. If we're going to do this, we're going to do it right. I'd like to see our float not only be the most magnificent one in the parade, but the most meaningful one as well."

"I'm still listening."

"I'm talking about the art referendum."

Beverly knew that Willie read the local papers a couple of times a week -- well, not really read, but at best, glanced over the headlines. Glanced-over was what he always did to political agendas as well. Mostly, he read the advertisements just to make sure that his was in line and effective. But he did notice the call for an Arts referendum.

"Just what is this sculpture thing Bev? And what's the referendum about? I've read a little about it, but you know me, I really don't get interested in stuff like that."

"We're getting people behind the idea of taking a piece of scruffy property up at Eisenhower Tunnel and make it a public domain for Art. There's a famous artist who's been living up at Coon Hill who wants to put an important sculpture just as you come out of the tunnel."

"He couldn't be too famous if he lives at Coon Hill."

Stoking Willie's ego, Beverly went on "he's only been up there so he could think. Willie, it could be wonderful. And we -- you, if you supported it and if it could become real -- would become known as an arts patron around here. You would be recognized as one of the primary influences on bringing 21st Century values to this county. Who knows? You might even get a plaque or something to hang up at work."

Always mindful of his business, Willie asked "And who are our enemies in this endeavor."

"That's the greatest part. There really aren't any enemies -- just uninformed people. We can use the Ullr float to teach – to get them informed. Really, Willie, there's no downside, and the possible upside is the recognition of Meinstrom's as a pioneer in bringing class to the county."

"Really?"

"Yeah, really. I imagine the float as being like the current county agenda up against a dumb Ullr myth. A sort of future against the past. Come on Willie. If you want me to show off my body, at least I can feel I did it for a cause -- and a cause that will probably be good for Meinstrom's not like it's not good already."

"Beverly you know I'm as easily swayed by you as any other male so, what the heck, whatever you say."

"What kind of float can we have, I mean, design, trailer all those things?"

"You take charge of it. I don't really care about the details. I'll pay you your normal hourly rate to get the thing done, designed, entered, and completed. I just want to win the parade competition and your presence on the float will tend to secure that result. Let me know what you need."

"Great Willie. Thanks a lot."

When she went home that night, Beverly called Darcy and told her about the float and Willie's acquiescence. Darcy would try to dig up some young artists who could help with the design and manufacture of the float but she wanted to know how they were going to make a model of a sculpture that nobody had ever seen. That was a really good question.

****

Beverly turned into a hard taskmaster. Within days of the discussion with Willie Meinstrom she was putting together a volunteer organization to build a float for the Ullr Fest. Michael was still hesitant to let Beverly make plans or promises that Philip would have to meet.

Philip responded to the emerging pressure for a sculpture design with renewed attention to detail and an eye to a public unveiling which is the bread, blood and spirit of any artist.

The first citizen to behold the model would be Beverly. For a few days she'd been thinking that she needed to talk to Michael about developments in general and invited him to dinner. Michael had been buried in the minutia of real estate at Eisenhower Tunnel and didn't mind the idea of a little dinner and conversation with the most beautiful woman in Colorado. Purely in the interest of art and metaphor, of course.

As Michael's Jeep pulled up in the driveway Beverly became sharply aware that he was a very comely man.

Beverly opened the door. "Come on in." She said, blushing slightly, realizing what she'd been thinking.

Michael's eyes were riveted to Beverly's. He dropped his hat. "Thanks. Smells delicious in here." He said. Picking up his hat and following Beverly in through the door he stumbled at the threshold. Beverly knew she had this effect on men sometimes and the blushing wasn't helping. She turned away to conceal her embarrassment and to give Michael a chance to recover. Now she knew his eyes were following the movement of her hips. She was beginning to perspire. The phone rang.

It was Darcy. "Hi. Bev, I was going out to the store for a few things and thought I would drop by if you're not busy."

Beverly took a long breath. She gave the situation a thought then said. "I've got something on the stove. Why don't you come on over. Michael's here and we'd love you to join us."

Beverly hung up the phone and turned to Michael. With her best matter of fact smile she said. "That was Darcy. She's going to join us for dinner."

"Good." Michael said. He was visibly relieved. "That's very good."

Before Darcy arrived, Beverly took care of her business with Michael. He still couldn't keep his eyes off of her but the atmosphere was no longer charged with possibilities.

"I feel like I'm making some progress toward securing access to the site at the tunnel." Michael said. "But it's slow. Darlene down at the county offices is trying to help."

"I know Darlene." Beverly said. "She's very good at her job. I feel sorry for her though. I'm told she used to be the object of a lot of gossip. Since her husband disappeared she hasn't done much else with her life but work at that job."

With that aside Beverly wanted to know when it would be possible for her to go meet the artist and see his work.

"Philip's in the final stages of work, and probably wouldn't like visitors." Michael said. "But I'll call him. He'll be adamantly opposed but he'll have to admit that his work of public art is finally going to have to meet its public. I also know..." Michael added almost against his will "...That Philip adores beauty more than most and will want to meet one of the most beautiful beings in the world."

"Thanks Michael." Beverly said simply. The doorbell rang. "That'll be Darcy."

So the next morning Michael and Beverly headed off to visit Philip at the quaint cabin-like place he and Theo had rented north of Silverthorne when they finally descended from Coon Hill. Philip had been working up a model out of clay.

"One of Philip's original conceptions was to have Dancing Star a pirouette." Michael explained. "For the sake of simplicity, he had given up this idea. But now, for the sake of gravity and the forces of nature, he's reconsidering it."

"It's a statue of a dancer?" Beverly asked.

"It's the creative power of humanity, I think but I'll let Philip tell you about metaphor. But, yes, she's a dancer. Looking up from here, If an axis were drawn vertically from her wrists through her ankles, not her toes, and if she were spun around this axis, even for 120 degrees, the area within the space circumscribed by her toes provided would enough base for the technological requirements. Whether 120 -- or 180 or even 360 -- degrees rotation would be aesthetically pleasing is the question Philip's dealing with right now."

"Like any artist he's irritated that he has to make a decisions based on something other than a perfect idea, but he's challenged by the new problem and its ultimate stability. He lost a lot of sleep rationalizing the needed rotation but I think for his high-speeding audience out of the tunnel, a figure that for 100 or so feet of tangential movement looks basically the same from every angle would be a better idea than the original which assumed that people would stop their cars en route to ski and look up at it."

Philip and Theo sketched several elevations from various spots along the roadway out of the tunnel. Driving out of the tunnel, it was not until you had traveled some 40-50 feet before the impact of the sculpture would be present. Since it was going to be placed 637 feet out, they drew an arc whose radii changed with proximity to the piece. Philip was trying to figure out how many degrees rotation around the axis was needed. Minimally, 250 degrees were needed. But that would only leave a 110 degree 'cavity' in the back of the piece. Why do this? No reason, certainly no aesthetic or structural reasons. Why not rotate her a full 360 degrees? Aesthetically, this would be a simpler form, and more balanced. Structurally, it would be easier to construct, and the base would be more than adequate. The problem with this idea, however, is that the end result would look more or less like a vase – not a dancer.

But, if, looking from the top, the vase was sliced sorta like a pizza except leaving the edges of the slices intact, the result would have a grand effect. Take five slices, and you would have, every seventy-two degrees, a dancer. Five dancers around an axis. So it was decided. Dancing Star would do a full pirouette, but with sections removed.

Philip explained it to Beverly, Michael and Theo.

"This is such a marvelous idea." Beverly said. "It's hard to imagine."

"It'll be as big as a six story building. You'll see the model when we get to there."

When they got to the cabin, Theo greeted them, and held his forefinger up to his mouth to indicate that they should talk quietly. Theo let Philip know that they were here, but Philip just kept working, so the others went out to the camp-fire pit they had constructed in the back yard.

"It's good to have company." Theo said, as he passed most welcome cups of hot coffee. "We've been sticking pretty close to here. Our van trips over to the tunnel have become fewer and farther between. Now the only concern is the model. Based on data from the bronze fabricator regarding the size of the supporting metal frame, and the quantity of material Philip can make a model to actual scale. Now that Beverly has him on a deadline he needs to construct a 1/18 scale model of Dancing Star that will be the final design for the tunnel."

"The model itself is modeled from a big hunk of clay but Philip's also experimenting with cement and bronze-wool.

Beverly was feeling more like she was part of the team. "How will he make something six stories high?" She asked, looking to Michael for confirmation that she had really understood how tall the sculpture would be.

"The final four foot model will be turned over to a bronze mold-form subcontractor who would digitize it. This computerized form will be the basis for all the rest of the construction. The mold-form subcontractor will make decisions regarding the number and size of partitions which can be transported and then fused together around an already constructed metal armature built on a base that's a two, 12 inch wide steel H-beams welded together. Eisenhower tunnel will be one of the limiting factors, 'cause we have to be able to transport the partitions through the tunnel -- unless, of course, we want to contract a helicopter, but I don't know if that will be in the budget. They'll build panels out of polyurethane, the same stuff used in this beer cooler. Then place sheets of a plasticized rubber around the structure, and vacuum it into place, that is just like putting a vacuum cleaner hose inside a plastic bag, the vacuum will suck the sheets up tight against the polyurethane. Then a chemical will be used to remove the polyurethane from the mold, and you have left a hollow model into which the bronze can be poured."

"Maybe I can make our model for the float out of beer coolers." Beverly speculated. "They're lightweight and cheap. Mr. Meinstrom will like that." She was still curious. "So the big sculpture will be made of a lot of different pieces?"

"It'll be a number of pieces but appear to be a single massive structure. The welds will be indiscernible. Then, the individual panels will be 'match-cast'. That's the key to making it look like one piece. They'll be poured side-by-side so that the material in each batch will match."

About twenty minutes into the conversation, Philip came out to the campfire where the others were brewing another pot of coffee. Michael rose, shook Philip's hand,

and introduced Beverly. As Philip approached within sight of Beverly, Theo noted Philip's usually distracted inward gaze reverse directions. He was imbibing her beauty. Theo turned his own attention in Beverly's direction. She was wearing slim, cross-country leggings and a tight wool sweater. Her cheeks were red in the cold air, and her hair was pulled back with a wool headband which covered her ears. Her face was magnificent. She was a goddess.

"I've been searching my heart and soul for a face that could compete with the beauty of these mountains and I've been wasting my time. She was over in Breckenridge all along. Michael why didn't you bring her to me sooner."

"Because you told us to leave you alone."

"You should have known better." Then Philip said to Beverly. "I've been staring at you haven't I?"

"Yes, you have." Beverly replied pointedly. She might have found anyone who talked in front of her like she wasn't there infuriating but there was something about Philip's rough honesty that made his motives seem different from other men.

"Yours is the image of Dancing Star." Philip appeased.

"But I'm not a dancer." Beverly accepted his apology.

"Where the overall form will be a permutation of dancing, the face I need is yours. The thing that we'll make will not be much like your face. The proportions of something that'll be seventy feet in the air have to be broadly stated and adjusted to the perspective of our mobile viewers but I have to have a vision of what I'm trying to communicate and now I know it's you."

Beverly was accustomed to the flattery of men and wasn't going to let herself be pushed over. "I came up to get an idea for the float we're designing for the Ullr Fest. Maybe I could get a look at what you're talking about?"

"Your float committee is our interface with the real world. I'd hope you'd want to see what you're supporting."

Michael and Theo returned to their drinks and conversation around the campfire. Philip welcomed Beverly into his 'studio' and pulled aside the damp sheet covering it. Beverly was speechless. It was almost as if some unearthly place had been transported to this cabin. The sculpture inside was beautiful.

When Philip began his animated description of placing her down at the tunnel, 77 feet tall, Beverly couldn't withhold her awe. "I've never met a genius before."

"I don't share your opinion." Philip said with resignation.

"How do you do it? How can you imagine such a project? What is it that makes it so easy for you to make a difference, and so hard for others, like me?"

"I'm different from others only in that my pursuits are out of the ordinary. Anyone who can do what he wants to do in life and get paid for it is a genius. I can envy someone's ability to get along in the real, workaday world. I fail when I don't know how to play those games correctly."

Beverly watched Philip making impressions on the clay sculpture with his strong hands as he was talking to her. She could tell that he studied her face with each glance in her direction.

"Do you mind if I feel the structure of your face." Philip asked. He wiped damp clay from his hands with a towel.

"No. I don't think so." Beverly replied. She lowered her eyes as she would when inviting a man to touch her. Philip's contact with her flesh was electrifying. It was simultaneously an investigation and a communication. Beverly experienced an infusion of cool clay from the skin surface of Philip's hands as if she were becoming the material of his art. His fingertips sought out every juncture of the bones of her face and followed the sinews to every seam and joint. Touching her jawline and then her shoulders his strength flared inside her brain. He could have broken her neck with a flick of his wrist. When Philip's hand's explored the links of her spine along the edge of her throat and followed under the neck of her sweater to the clavicles Beverly clenched her teeth, tightened her thighs, and held her breath.

When she opened her eyes, Philip had returned to the sculpture. He appeared to be reproducing every instant of the exploration of her body on the surface of the clay. He was in a distant world of his own. Then as if remembering an obligation he looked up from his work.

"Thank you." He said. "I wasn't sure that Dancing Star would be beautiful enough but now I am."

Out by the fire Michael was catching up on the news from camp. "I'm impressed that you've been able to keep a regulated temperature for Philip's work with clay. To be honest I expected that you would have had to come down to a more civilized environment a long time ago."

"It's been a trial but that's what Philip wanted it to be. We're close to the end now."

Beverly wasn't sure how long she watched Philip work in silence but after a while she rejoined Michael and Theo at the campfire. "I guess we'd better head back now. I think I have a good enough idea of Dancing Star to finish the float."

****

Michael's cell phone rang just after he took Beverly home. Barry sounded out-of-sorts. "Michael, I'm under arrest. Can you come to the police station? You'll find out about it once you get here."

"Sure, be there in about ten minutes." "What in the world?" he wondered as he steered the Wagoneer toward town.

Michael entered the interrogation room. Barry Hollister was waiting there under arrest. Detective Chance was sitting across the table and a uniformed officer was standing nearby. It was late-afternoon and stubble had begun to appear on Barry's face. His clothes were obviously expensive but casual, if a tad rumpled. Michael wondered if Detective Chance might relish the experience of grilling the rich boy from back East.

Michael gave Barry his most reassuringly firm pat on the shoulder and pulled up another brown folding chair.

Detective Chance said, as if for the record, "Mr. Hollister is under arrest and has requested a lawyer be present at this interrogation."

Michael took up the official tone, "What's the charge?"

Detective Chance read quickly from a charge sheet near at hand, "Statutory rape, contributing to the delinquency, reckless endangerment, kidnapping, rape, sexual battery, and sodomy."

Michael tried to keep the astonishment from showing on his face. He turned to Barry who was vigorously shaking his head. Michael wasn't a criminal lawyer. This was way out of his range.

Detective Chance continued, "Mr. Hollister, a neighbor, Jane Frampton called the police around 8:30 this morning reporting that a naked female was seen wandering, apparently dazed, in the exterior rear premises of a residence at 443 S. Hampton. Is that your address Mr. Hollister?"

Barry protested, "I left before dawn this morning."

"Then it is your address. When the police arrived they found the doors locked and an incoherent woman's voice answering from a room in the back. They forced the back door and found a sixteen year old female, Cynthia Donahue, partially dressed and nearly unconscious sitting on a bed in your residence. She reported that she had been drugged and assaulted."

Barry stiffened and his hands clenched into fists but he maintained his composure, "Oh God. Is she OK?"

"OK would be relative in this case, Mr. Hollister. The medical examiner found no evidence of semen on her body but reports that her vagina and anus were abraded. He expects that further testing will confirm traces of phenobarbital in her blood. Her wrists and ankles were bruised and 'open for business' had been written in ink, like a tattoo, on her buttocks within the last twenty four hours. I don't think I'm putting too fine a point on this Mr. Hollister, Miss Donahue names you as her assailant."

There was a look of remote disbelief in Barry's eyes. For a moment it seemed as if he would be unable to answer the charge. It shouldn't be possible to find a context, a shared world, in which Barry Hollister, scion of one of Connecticut's most prominent families could explain to a fat police detective that he didn't sexually brutalize a young woman who was his student athlete and friend. But even in the purest, most noble Hollister spirit there might exist dark regions where images of beautiful, young, buttocks can attach themselves, find context and grow in meaningfulness.

Barry collected himself and faced up to the explanation, "I coach a volleyball team. Cynthia is my best blocker. I knew she had a crush on me but that was all. She knocked on my door last night--I don't know--11:30? She said she was having trouble at home. I let her in. I know her mother, Mary Donahue. I told her she ought to go home or at least call. Cynthia said her mother had caught some of her friends dressing in her mother's clothes and necking in the master bedroom. She said they had a big fight -- that nobody knew where she was--that she needed to talk to me. And, damn my stupidity, I let her stay. I let her gaze into my eyes and tell me about her little problems and dreams. I let her shower and change into my bathrobe. I let her have a glass of wine. And I kissed her good night on her forehead. I was stupid. I had had too much wine myself. But she went to sleep on the couch and that's where she was when I left the house at six this morning. I didn't have sex with her. I didn't rape her and I didn't leave any messages on her ass."

Detective Chance said, "I find it hard to believe the part about the tattoos myself, but you admit you were drunk and behaved inappropriately with a minor."

"I wasn't drunk."

"There was no forced entry, into the residence I mean, and no indication of anyone else on the premises. Somebody had a lot of fun at Miss Donahue's expense last night and, Mr. Hollister, it looks to me like you're the one."

Chance told Michael that he could bail Barry out in the morning.

Michael Lovell turned his Waggoneer off of River Road onto Tarnshore drive. No one at the Donahue place had returned his calls in twenty four hours and he was going to take a chance that they would answer the door if he was there in person. They couldn't avoid a confrontation with Barry's attorneys forever but Michael wanted to talk to Mary and Cynthia now, unofficially and in the spirit of a common search for the truth.

He found the third house on the right and scanned the balconies overlooking the drive. In his heart he was hoping to see a greeting from one of the French windows and an indication that this was all a mistake. The windows were dark and empty.

Michael knocked on the imposing front door, waited and knocked again. A tall girl in a big sweater, jeans and heavy boots answered the door. This must be the star volleyball player or a member of a family of volleyball players. Her dark features were too strong to be pretty at her age but interesting and attractive. She would grow into a very beautiful woman. Michael introduced himself and asked, "Are you Cynthia Donahue?"

The girl pulled door open enough to see out then hesitated. She looked Michael over for signs of who he might be or what he might want and answered anyway, "Yea. I'm Cynthia."

"I'm a friend of Barry Hollister's. May I talk to you for a minute?"

Cynthia closed the screen door. "There's nothing to say."

"Barry says he didn't rape you."

"He didn't have to do that."

"He didn't have to--?"

"Drug me and rape me. I wanted him to notice me. I walked by the door of the locker room to let him see me almost naked so he'd think about me. And he did. He said he loved me and I loved him. I would have given him anything he wanted. He didn't have to do it that way."

"But you were unconscious when you were attacked."

"I remember where I was and what was happening to me. I wouldn't have told them what he did, but I wasn't thinking straight when they found me. I trusted him and he's a bastard. My father's going to be in tomorrow and you better keep your friend in that jail 'cause when he gets out my Daddy's going to blow his head off."

Cynthia opened the door again. Michael took a chance and stepped inside.

"Maybe we should talk to your mother?" He said, wishing to move the conversation off the subject of private vengeance. Michael glanced over his shoulder back toward the drive. He sincerely hoped that her Father hadn't taken an earlier flight.

"She's out. I think she's talking to a lawyer."

"Did Barry Hollister really say he loved you?"

"Yea. Cynthia said, "Barry wrote me a letter. He asked me to come by his house. Then look what he did to me. You want me to show you this tattoo?" Cynthia turned her back away from the door and began pulling down the seat of her jeans. "And it's not even pretty."

Michael wanted to see the tattoo but he needed to see the letter. He grasped a belt loop of Cynthia's jeans to impede their downward progress and said, "Can you show me the letter?"

"The police have it." Cynthia said. And on the rocky shore of that simple statement dashed the frail vessel of Michael's hope for an easy answer to Barry's predicament.

****

Later that day, Cynthia changed her story and refused to testify to a charge of rape against Barry. Detective Chance was left with circumstantial evidence of illegal drug use involving a minor but couldn't make anything stick.

There was no evidence against Barry. Nor was there evidence of any other attacker. Barry was generally assumed to be guilty but set free. He was shaken to the roots by the suspicion, by the hostility and by the lack of support from people he had considered to be his friends. He had never in his life been actually vulnerable or known what it was like to feel despised. Barry's dad, Nelson Hollister flew in as soon as he received word of Barry's arrest. When the charges were dropped they closed the condo and left town together. Without Barry to help put things together there was no possibility of further investigation.

At the airport in Denver, Barry kissed Beverly goodbye and said they should stay in touch. Michael was a lawyer and accustomed being a paid friend but he really had come to like Barry. Michael wanted to see Barry off and also see if there was anything left of the Hollister connection to Philip's project. There wasn't.

Driving back up toward the Continental Divide Michael said as a matter of fact, "I still don't think he did it."

Beverly replied, "He might have done it. He would have done it. He wanted to do it. What difference does it make? He said that the best part of being a girls' volleyball coach was the smell of all that damp, musty girl in the huddle."

"Did Barry actually say that?"

"He didn't say it to me of course. But Andrew Wolltrip told me what he said. Why are women always such fools?"

Michael didn't venture an answer. "Wolltrip, huh? I've never known if he could be trusted." he thought. They drove silently and uncomfortably through the Eisenhower Tunnel, past an unremarkable parcel of undeveloped land on the right and on to Breckenridge.

Michael wondered what would become of the Art Domain Department without Barry.

****

Darcy was having dinner at Beverly's house.

As they brought their salads and pasta into the living room Beverly said, "There's nothing left for me. I don't know where I'll be going."

Darcy took a seat on the sofa with her salad bowl balanced on her knee. "Aren't you involved in a new arts commission?" Darcy asked. "You sounded pretty excited about it talking to Nelson Hollister."

"He turned out to be a shit head. He acted like I was somehow to blame for Barry's humiliation. I don't want anything more to do with any of them."

"I'm not asking about Nelson or Barry. I'm talking about you and the arts commission. I know you were involved because of Barry but I thought you were interested because of yourself."

"I'm just so disappointed. I'm just so lost. I was connected to the project through Barry. He gave me a lot of inspiration."

"When I was a girl I thought I was smart enough to take care of myself but I still ended up getting drunk and letting some pimply faced jerk pump me in the back seat of a Dodge."

Beverly nodded in bitter agreement and appended her own recollection. "A Ford." She said.

"I liked dating." Darcy continued. "I liked the excitement of meeting someone and not knowing what was going to happen and thinking that my whole life could change because I had met this person. And I liked men but I began to realize that what I didn't like was sex. To have these adventures and relationships I had to let these guys take me. I just grew tired of getting it. I was tired of having to let that other half of the population pound me before they'd let me hang with them. But what was I to do?

"So you're a lesbian."

"I'm a woman who remains open to experiences. So, put Barry out of your mind and think about what you could do for the art project without him. That's what I'd do.

"You're right. I can't let my life be torn up by Barry's failure. But I miss him so much."

Beverly began to weep. When Darcy put a consoling arm around her it felt so warm and right. Beverly nestled against Darcy and let herself break down completely. She felt safe and confident that Darcy's embrace wasn't motivated by desire. She thought of all the times she had turned to men for comfort and got screwed instead. She was soothed to be in the patient arms of a woman. Darcy kissed the tears from Beverly's cheeks as they continued to flow and held her until they had run dry.

Beverly wanted to say thank you for these rare moments of peace. She didn't know how to say how much she appreciated Darcy's help and comfort so she gave her a big kiss on the lips. She realized that she was mixing sexual pleasure with friendship and wondered if Darcy would think less of her. She wondered if Darcy would think she was falling back into old patterns of offering access to her body as a reward. The deep kiss that Darcy returned convinced Beverly that she had been accepted.

In the days that followed Beverly began to sort out the overlay of her romantic involvement with Barry with her commitment to his political interests. She had been confused -- no, not confused as much as bewildered...as if there's a difference.

No doubt, Barry's relationship to her had had an effect on her hormones. She had thought she should fall in love with Barry, but she was afraid to. He came from a different mold than her. He was a trust-fund child and she was a shop girl. Like in an old movie. His family wealth gave him an aura of power that was mixed up with his personality. In her trusting, naive innocence Beverly was overwhelmed. The thought of being loved by him had flattered her but now she began to realize that always in the back of her mind had been the feeling that she would have all that money if she had Barry.

Barry had been at the same time loving and preoccupied... preoccupied with the commissioner's role, the volleyball team and, primarily this sculpture project. In the course time from Barry's accounts, she'd become convinced that the project was probably important. But...but Beverly didn't have a political bone in her body. For her, the sculpture was interesting, but it had no relevance to her life. For Barry, it was a challenge and inspiration, the extent of which was incomprehensible to Beverly. She loved and desired Barry, and her desire had stimulated a love for his interests, whether she understood them or not. Lifted by Darcy's friendship and advice Beverly set out to make this interest her own. She wanted to stop waiting for someone else to set the boundaries of her life.

The first step was to be sure that Barry's proposal didn't fade away because he had abandoned it. Beverly needed a friend and ally that could connect her to local politics. She called Andrew Wolltrip at his office and asked him to meet her for lunch at the Lodgepole.

"God you look great" he said as they headed into the dining room. "Haven't seen you in a while and I'm still wilting at your sheer beauty."

She didn't withdraw as he bent down and lightly kissed her cheek.

"How's work at the county offices?"

"Oh, 'bout the same." Andrew said off hand. "Listen Bev my ego kept me from questioning when you might call and ask me to lunch but I knew that thing with Hollister was going to be a bust."

"Thanks Andy but I don't want to pick up where we left off right now. I've changed and there's a lot I need to sort out."

"There's plenty of time." Andrew said. "Just call me soon."

Beverly noted his self-confident presumption and wondered if he had always been so arrogant about predicting her behavior. "I want you to help me fill Barry's place on the arts issues."

Andrew almost gasped. He smiled curiously and said. "That's not at all what I was expecting you to say."

Beverly was annoyed. "I know. Everybody expects me to say what they expect but I want to see this through."

Andrew tried to be serious. "There's going to be a special meeting next week to discuss the future of Hollister's arts committee, but we expect it to die."

"Fill me in on what's going on."

"Do you want me to start at the beginning?"

"There's plenty time.

"Hollister made a request to get the county commissioners to lend political and economic support to an arts committee whose initial focus would be a sculpture of some kind. The result would be a referendum in the January elections, asking whether the constituency was willing to found, then fund, a quasi-municipal arts body. This would be the first step in acquiring local, grass roots support. My role was getting the notice of the meeting publicized and planning an agenda. We didn't expect too large of a turnout among the various constituencies. Hollister said a lot of bull about truth, beauty and whatnot that put everybody to sleep but I was trying to put the proposal on a business-like footing."

"How do you really feel about the project?" Beverly asked with a sweet hesitant manner that wouldn't force Andrew to a quick conclusion.

"You know what I and the whole town feel about Hollister." Andrew looked up into Beverly's deep blue eyes, stole a quick glance down to a peek of cleavage at the vee of her blouse and changed course. "Oh, I think it's probably a good idea, but I doubt the county will ever fund it. I mean, taxes are so high already, just to keep ordinary maintenance and services in order. All the department heads are planning budgets for next year, and I'm sure that, as usual, there won't be any funds left over. On the outside, the project will get approval pending funding."

Beverly unconsciously tugged at her top button and asked. "What does that mean?"

"Only that it'll receive the blessings of the commissioners with no obligation to follow through because the funds won't be there."

"Can it be funded from the outside -- from some other source?"

"Probably, but that would require a huge amount of coordination, permissions, leases, contractual responsibilities and, ultimately, the effort would probably get lost in reams of paperwork."

"Andrew, you're the paperwork genius west of the Mississippi. I bet if you favored the project, you'd have no problem producing the right proposals and memos and documents. Am I right?"

"I'm flattered Beverly but I'm not anxious to take on a lot of work on a project that's probably going to fail anyway."

Without thinking Beverly put her hand on Andrew's knee, looked straight into his eyes again and said simply, "It would be wonderful if you'd help us. We admire people who take a stand for things they really believe in don't we -- I mean regardless of the personal cost."

"Who else have you been talking to about this?" Andrew asked.

"Nobody you'd know. Darcy Rios-Doria. She's a girl I met through Barry. She's been a lot of help to me."

Andrew hadn't seen Darcy since she disappeared from the bar at Tony's. The prospect of working closely with these two beauties, having them be good friends while serving his passion, severally and perhaps jointly, fired Andrew's enthusiasm for modern art beyond all imagining.

They finished a pleasant lunch and Andrew asked if they'd do it again next week. "Sure" Beverly answered. "Just let me know when. I'd like to see you again soon"

"And bring along your friend Darcy." Andrew added. "We can talk about art."

With that, they left and Beverly was convinced that Andrew would support the project. She was sure that he hadn't misinterpreted the friendly squeeze of his knee.

At the next BOCC meeting, a week later, Andrew introduced Beverly as a new volunteer leader of the petition drive asking for a referendum on the project. She had prepared all the necessary documents and had enough names. Darcy turned out to have a surprising head for legal language and had assisted with the wording of the proposal for the referendum.

The referendum propositions were:

1. That there should be an arts committee at the department level of the county commissioners which receives funding from taxes for the creation of a public domain of art, or

2. That there should be an arts committee at the department level of the county commissioners whose funding is not part of the county budget, or

3. That there should not be an arts committee at the department level of the county commissioners

The BOCC voted that the referendum election would be in late January, at a time to be decided at the next meeting after all the formal documents were prepared. And they named Beverly chairperson of the, temporary for now, Department of Art Domains.

It had been more than two months since Michael began his commuting life from Colorado to New York. He worked in Georgetown for a week or two when he was needed and then flew back for a stint in his office on Wall Street. Felicity said their lives hadn't become bi-coastal. It was only a coast and a half. Her good humor and independent spirit had made it all possible. She was always busy on her next domestic project and entangled in commitments to volunteer work. The girls were doing well in school and Michael called them almost every day when he was away. He spent two weeks during the Christmas vacation in New York.

Felicity had been trying to be patient and supportive but Michael suspected that she had brought her mother's influence on line to push the work in Colorado to a conclusion.

Phone calls and meetings with Jeff Holmes had established the feasibility of support for Philip's Colorado Project from the Community Arts Initiative. Over a lunch or two at Alphonso's Elsa Horowitz had forged a relationship with Barbara Simpson, the chair of the foundation's Artist Advisory Committee. Now Elsa was on her way out to Colorado. She had been working to set up a meeting between Beverly Moore at the Department of Art Domains and Barbara Simpson. She thought Philip should join in so that the aesthetic and community issues could all be addressed at the same time. Michael wasn't sure that Barbara was the right contact but it was time to play the hand.

Michael called the Friday night before Felicity and Elsa were scheduled to fly out from New York. Felicity was packing and Elsa was spending the night with the girls.

"So, how's life really like in the frozen backwoods of Colorado?" Felicity asked.

"Where I'm living is not exactly backwoods. Coon Hill is backwoods, as you'll see if the weather holds and I can get you up there, but not here. I've described the place I'm living in but you've just got to see it to appreciate its enchantment. It's rustic, quaint and homey but I'm sure you could turn it into a fashion forward show piece in a few weeks. You've got to see it."

"We're on our way. I talked to Sherrie last week, and she said she wouldn't mind coming over to keep the girls if you'd introduce her to the new tennis pro at the club."

"Done. She really wants to meet that bum? Christ. She really has no class."

Felicity laughed. "That's how I met you wasn't it. All of a sudden, you sound like my dad."

"Your dad always said you were lucky to get me."

"That's what he told you."

"Fel, I miss you more than you could ever know. I want to share -- or reveal to you the part of me that has always loved these mountains. I'll see you at DIA tomorrow and I really do look forward to seeing you sweetheart."

"And Mother."

"What?"

"You'll be seeing Mother too."

"I'll be seeing both of you tomorrow."

Michael had hired a cleaning company to come in and rejuvenate the cabin on Friday, wash the bed linens, dust, vacuum, clean up the kitchen. Then, Saturday morning he took off for Denver about 10:30. Felicity and Elsa were arriving at Stapleton at 2:15 from LaGuardia. As soon as he arrived in Denver he had the Wagoneer washed, and headed to the Tattered Cover bookstore to pick up some books on "The Law and Art", "Commissioner Government", and "Low-level Federal Bureaucracies."

He pulled into the Stapleton parking lot about 1:45. The arrival/departure monitors indicated that Felicity's flight would be about 15 minutes late, so he ducked into one of the "Skycap" bars along the concourse and had a couple of drinks while thumbing through his books.

The arrival of Felicity's flight was announced at gate 31, and as Michael headed to the gate, he looked down at himself. He had on corduroy trousers, mid-calf-high leather boots, and a plaid, teal colored flannel shirt. He was wondering how this attire would suit Fel's taste as he looked up and saw her walking through the deplaning portal.

Obviously Felicity and Elsa had been shopping for just the right combination of taste and ruggedness which, from their East Coast perspective, would be the right fit for a first class flight to the wilderness of Denver. Felicity was dressed in a relatively low profile pair of plum herringbone patterned corduroy trousers, a pink, cotton turtleneck, a hounds tooth jacket and some taupe calfskin boots. She was composed and beautiful. Elsa was wearing a bright, crisply starched, country and western outfit complete with rose embroidered shirt, fringed jacket and cowboy boots. She was a woman who did things her own way. Michael marveled that they were mother and daughter.

He took Elsa's carry on. Her new leather jacket squeaked as he hugged her shoulders. He gave Felicity a real welcoming kiss. In all these years he had never stopped feeling warmed and aroused in greeting her.

"God you feel good." he whispered as they turned back to walk back through concourse C.

Elsa volunteered a summary of the last few hours. "Well, the flight was delayed out of LaGuardia. Some maintenance nonsense. For the prices they charge you'd think they could buy planes that would fly without any trouble. The kids are with Sherrie. What does a tennis pro have to do with the arrangements? Do we have a plan?"

"I'm open to suggestions." Michael said. "We can either have dinner here in Denver or head on up to Georgetown."

Felicity squeezed Michael's had. "Denver is just another big city."

"It didn't look that big from the air." Interjected Elsa.

"It's not big compared to a mountain." Felicity defended Michael's newest residence, "and I came here to see my man in the mountains. I'm anxious to get on up to Georgetown.

"Whatever that is." scoffed Elsa.

"Great."

They loaded the luggage into the Wagoneer, and headed out I-70. En route to Georgetown, Michael and Felicity talked about the kids, the club, her life, his life, the difference between Manhattan and the West. Michael, respectful of Felicity, still couldn't hide his enthusiasm about these friggin' mountains. They just couldn't be ignored! And as the Wagoneer ascended beyond the front-range into the mountains, Michael became more animated. One hand on the wheel, the other pointing out the sights of Idaho Springs, gold mining sites, remnants of late 19th century cabins, and most importantly, the mountains.

Felicity was receptive. She was on holiday, and from her perspective, Michael's enthusiasm for the mountains differed from his enthusiasm for the divers in Acapulco only in degree, not in kind. Michael felt like he was on assignment, and typical of him, he threw himself into the job. He knew that Felicity, Barbara and Elsa needed to be convinced of the aesthetic and social significance of his work.

They took the turnoff from I-70 into Georgetown, and as they did Michael wondered if Elsa felt like she was in a time warp. At the intersection were a couple of convenience stores and signs pointing to chain motels. Michael sensed her apprehension and kept driving. Beyond the intersection was a town. The town he'd begun to love. Homes built in the late 1800's had become craft shops and galleries for tourist focused mountain art.

They turned off 1st Street, onto a gravel road which wended its way along the river to his cabin. It was late afternoon, and the sun had just begun to disappear behind the Continental Divide.

As they pulled into the driveway, Felicity finally said quietly, "How quaint. Michael, you must love it here."

Michael's Garden of Eden wasn't impressing his Eve. They unloaded Felicity's luggage into the second bedroom where Michael had transferred his clothes. Elsa was settled into the master bedroom if master was not too authoritative a term to apply to a room so simple and congenial. Michael set about to get a roaring fire going in the fireplace. He put a Bach prelude on the stereo and encouraged Fel to relax. She was edgy after traveling most of the day with her mother.

He'd bought some cheap California champagne, the only kind he could find at the local liquor store, the day before. He opened it, went out on the balcony, and yelled for Fel to join him for a few minutes while Elsa was changing out of their traveling clothes.

Two hundred-fifty days a year, the sunsets from Georgetown were so photogenic that you had to be a supremely incompetent photographer, which Michael was, not to get a shot that could be in National Geographic. The other 115 days were those when Georgetown was absolutely socked-in you couldn't even see the end of the street, much less the mountains. Today was one of the clear days. There were just enough clouds over the divide to prismatically refract the setting sun into a blazing hemisphere. As Felicity joined Michael on the balcony, the setting sun spewed its rays up and away at all angles from beyond the Continental Divide, leaving in the fading orange and purple sky a dark space for night, evening and starlight.

Michael hoped that Felicity would see from his posture and the absence of gesture that he was absorbed, and wanted her to be too, in the holiness of the scene. They sipped their champagne silently. She moved over closer to him. Both his elbows were propped on the balcony rail, his hands cupped under his chin, and he was staring off into the distant west. She turned and looked too. It really was beautiful.

At Michael's shoulder Felicity whispered softly, "It's quiet." The only sound was that of the stream, rushing over and among the rocks.

As the sky turned from orange to purple to royal blue, a chill forced them inside toward the warmth of the fire, now roaring in the fireplace and accompanied by Elsa clinking in the kitchen.

After Elsa had gone to bed. Felicity and Michael snuggled in front of the fireplace for an hour before going to bed where they made up for several weeks lost time.

The next morning, Dawn broke through a cold white mist that was more frozen air than snow. Michael watched the expanding daylight through the kitchen window, holding the coffee pot beneath the faucet with his right hand while rubbing the sleep from his eyes with his left. Felicity was still asleep in the spare bedroom.

He turned off the faucet and poured water over coffee grounds, dying to expend themselves. While the coffee brewed, he weighed whether to stoke the fire -- the same fire in front of which he and Felicity had snuggled the night before. The mere thought made him smile. Absentmindedly, he walked toward the hearth.

The fireplace was opposite the bar which separated the den from the kitchen. This whole cabin had been designed by someone who valued scenery over heat-efficiency. Large, plate-glass windows everywhere. Poor for insulation but rich for anesthetics -- which led Michael's thoughts to the day's agenda. Elsa had paid for a ticket to bring Barbara Simpson out to gauge the local support for large scale public art. Beverly Moore was to meet Barbara at the airport in Denver this morning and bring her to the Moose Top Lodge in Breckenridge. Michael, Felicity and Elsa would join them later in the afternoon. Michael insisted that Theo bring Philip down for that meeting. If Elsa was going to bring her influence to bear on the Community Arts Initiative and Barbara in New York he wanted them to have the confidence and support of the whole Colorado organization.

After breakfast, they would head up to the Eisenhower Tunnel to meet Theo and Philip who would drive up from Silverthorne. Everyone would walk the site of the proposed sculpture then drive over to Breckenridge to join Beverly for lunch.

Michael stoked the coals, and their warmth was welcome. He was anxious to get underway, but he put on a new log knowing it would burn down before they were ready to leave.

The coffee was brewed by now, so he went back to the kitchen, got a full mug for himself, and one for Felicity. He took her cup into her, gently shook her and awakened her from her satisfied slumber.

"Fel. I love you. Good morning. Here's some coffee."

He pecked her cheek with a kiss and waited for her to wake up.

"Christ, what time is it?"

"It's already almost 6:30, 8:30 in New York. Here, have some coffee."

Rubbing her eyes, she slowly sat up in bed and Michael watched her eyes survey the room while she oriented herself.

"As soon as you're ready, there's a great fire in the fireplace. I promise, Fel, once you get out of bed, there's a world out there dying to introduce itself to you."

"Just give me a minute to get situated. Big difference between waking up here and waking up in Manhattan. Give me a second to get my wits together."

She sipped the coffee, noticing the difference in taste from what she had at home. "Great coffee. What's the brand."

"It's not the brand, but the water. Water here's pure as the souls who sip it."

"Really! Interesting comparison."

"I'm going back into the den. Meet ya there."

"O.k. Just let me get oriented."

Michael headed back to the den, put yet another log on the fire, and sat down on the leather bench in front of the fireplace. In a few minutes, Fel came out and joined him.

"Michael, back in New York I might dismiss this as quaint but I really do love the beauty out the window."

Felicity and Michael and been staring silently at the fireplace for quite some time. They drank their coffee and watched coals form from the logs while the sun was awakening, illuminating the mountains. The dawn was indescribable -- always witnessed as if for the first time. On the other side of the circular driveway stood a giant, blue spruce, barely distinguishable from the horizon at this early hour. Gradually materializing at the base of the spruce was a rotund figure with short cylindrical, handless arms affixed at right angles to a nearly spherical body. Michael thought the Martians were advancing up his driveway. Felicity said, "Mother?"

The door opened and with a crunch and swirl of snow Elsa entered. She was wearing innumerable layers of cold weather apparel. "Just testing my insulation," Elsa explained as she fumbled to close the door wearing two pairs of mittens. "Now I'm ready for a journey to the top of the world."

Michael was able to extract Elsa from enough clothing to fit her into the back of the Waggoneer by promising that not one stitch, hair, feather or kapok of warm clothing would be left behind. They packed Elsa's reserve winter gear, coffee and Michael's notes for the meeting with Barbara Simpson and they were off to the Continental Divide. Exiting the west portal of the Eisenhower Tunnel and scanning the snow banks to the right for signs of human life revealed a small lean man in a heavy, blue parka scooting across the packed snow mounds with the thoughtless ease of a New Yorker hailing a cab and getting to his destination faster. It had to be Theo Boudreaux. Michael steered onto the clear parking area. He expected to see Philip emerge from behind at any moment but Theo approached the Wagoneer alone.

"Good morning all." Theo said. "It's a beautiful day for a stroll."

"Where's Philip?" asked Michael with a hint of concern in his voice.

"He's still working in Silverthorne."

Michael's concern turned to annoyance. "People from all of the civilized world have come up here at great trouble and expense to talk to him."

"That's what I've been telling him for two days."

"I want you to meet my mother Elsa Horowitz." Felicity interjected as Theo angled his snowshoes into the rear and himself into the back seat.

"Sure." Theo said. "We met at the wedding."

"You're probably thinking of my sister."

"Oh yes. I met Blanch. And she's the mother of ...."

"Lucinda Goldwin."

"Who dances the ..."

"Lindy Hop. And likes artsy men with no visible means of support."

"Now I remember."

"I thought you might."

"That was a great weekend."

"So where the Hell is Philip?" Michael asked again, as they cruised the icy highway down toward Breckenridge.

Theo leaned to the front seat and replied. "Philip, without a moment's thought, said flatly that he wouldn't come."

"Does he think he can afford this work without our support?" Elsa asked. "It's as simple as that. Does he think he can sit up here in these 'ivory' mountains and ignore commerce with his audience?"

Theo tried to deflect Elsa's pique. "He's played this game before. I don't know what's bothering him now."

Elsa was persistent. "Don't you think we should find out what he's thinking? Can we put our fannies on the line for his art if his principles, whatever they might be, are going to be more important than the project? A little reality wouldn't hurt here."

"Philip wouldn't think there's a difference between reality and principles." Theo added. "He doesn't believe we can even ask a question about it. He's got a point. If his purpose is to elevate, or as he says I persistently misstate it, exonerate man, it's morally reprehensible if not self-contradictory, to get down to a common level. That would be an admission that the work isn't elevating, that it isn't art."

Elsa dismissed Theo's characterization of her level of involvement as common. "I wouldn't want to be too anti-elevating." She said. "But we'll eventually need his cooperation here. Over from his mountain retreat if not from his principles."

"I agree." Michael said. "But for today Philip's absence, rather than being harmful, will have to be leveraged in our favor. We'll have to make his absence into amplification of the significance of the project."

Michael, Felicity, Theo and Elsa approached the entrance of the Moose Top restaurant and bar tramping the snow from their boots on the grating outside the door and looking inside for Beverly Moore and Barbara Simpson. With the ski season in high gear the place was filled with clattering aggregations of diners and drinkers all on a boisterous holiday schedule. For a few days they would eat when they were hungry, drink when they were thirsty and ski when they weren't too gorged or drunk to stay upright on the slopes.

Beverly and Barbara were waiting at a large empty table near the back room. Michael was pleased to see them engaged in friendly and animated conversation. Beverly's leadership of the Department of Art Domains and enthusiasm for community art would be more important to Barbara Simpson than Philip's philosophies.

Barbara Simpson greeted Elsa with a broad smile and was introduced to Michael and Felicity. Michael introduced Theo and they all shuffled chairs and sat with Barbara at the center of the group's attention. She was a lean, animated woman entering into a well-tended middle age. She would have been a fascinating beauty in her youth. Michael was thinking that maybe she still was.

Barbara welcomed Elsa to the table with a genuine enthusiasm that made it really clear why she had been chosen to represent the Community Arts Initiative to an influential patron.

"Thanks for bringing me out here." Barbara said. "What a great spot. It's beautiful."

"Considering the cost of lunch in New York," Elsa replied, "it's also a bargain."

"But I expected to see Philip Alathon with you."

Since he was anticipating the question, Theo took over. "In all truth, Philip was drawn between coming to this meeting and sustaining the momentum of a significant phase of his work. He sends his apologies."

Behind Barbara's shoulder Elsa rolled her eyes and received a sharp scowl from Felicity.

Theo continued. "Philip's aware of the inconvenience but thought that if he interrupted his train of ideas right now something of it's excellence might be lost in the process. As he put it, a hen can't let her eggs get cold."

"I'm sure it is cold up there." Barbara said glancing over her shoulder at a suddenly heavy snow fall. "I'm familiar with Philip's style. I expected him to say flatly that he wouldn't come and then add a tirade about art critics -- or commentaries on anything for that matter. 'My work speaks for itself.' He's said more than once. 'Excellence needs no explanation.'

I know Philip's opinions about explanations. We served on a panel more years ago than I like to admit. At the University of Somewhere in the Mid-West. I can't remember now. But when the art critic on the panel declared that he wasn't interested in looking at a work of art if the artist couldn't articulate a coherent theory of the work Philip shouted an interruption saying that he wouldn't listen to a critic who couldn't show a coherent body of artwork. Thereafter every time the critic spoke Philip put his head in his hands and sang 'Waltzing Matilda' quietly to himself. It was completely childish and totally effective. Or so we all thought. We were a lot younger then."

"If you know Philip," Theo continued, "then you know how difficult he sometimes makes things for himself. He's been camping in the mountains in winter for instance. But you also know that he follows through with his ideas and most importantly keeps his word once he commits to a project. But I must say that this piece of art isn't, shall we say 'typical' of Philip. Rather than being dynamically destructive, outrageous, ridiculous or incomprehensible, this one will will be, for lack of a better word, beautiful. Philip's new work will be pleasing, and, as Santayana remarked, if it's pleasing, it's justified and grounded in human nature."

Barbara nodded in agreement. "I have to tell you that Jeff Holmes inquired why the foundation should consider a request from an artist who didn't have the courtesy to ask. Of course in our line of work, nothing should seem, unusual. But one thing I noticed right away was that it wasn't Philip himself who applied for the grant. We usually expect the presentation of an artist's project along with the application. But once we understood that Michael was his attorney and also the son-in-law of Elsa, we understood that an organization was already being put into place that had significant support."

"I've been telling Barbara about the referendum in January to establish a Department of Art Domains." Beverly said.

Michael opened a portfolio of photos, news clippings and

magazine articles about Philip and began to outline their agenda. Beverly would describe what the need was vis-a-vis the Summit County electorate and the referendum results, and Theo would stand in for Philip on aesthetic matters. Michael had already realized that Barbara knew as much about Philip's past work than anyone at the table.

Theo began the presentation. "Barbara, as you said, Philip believes this work is self-justifying. As we interpret the CAI's bylaws, project funding requires 'a project that is grounded in the historicity of Art or that leads to a clearer human understanding of excellence in art'. For Philip there's no separation of art from ethics. Philip believes that art leads to an appreciation of the good, without which there is no value."

Michael took up the thought, "Barbara, have you ever been to the Rocky Mountains before."

"No. When I want to get out of the city I vacation on the sea."

"Folks traveling along Interstate 70, some four million of them a year, not only will have an opportunity, but they'd have to be blind not to notice a piece placed at the western end of Eisenhower Tunnel. They will be a captive audience. Art, excellence, beauty, and ultimately a moral consciousness will be promulgated. This is important and appropriate for CAI funding. With all the controversy over art's funding this is a chance to clear the air. This is art in its full historical bloom."

"Well yes," Elsa interjected, "Barbara and I have discussed Philip's work on several occasions. He's been successful in the art community but we've never known where to place him. He's not an outsider artist, avant-garde or in the mainstream either. He didn't start out hounding the important galleries trying to place his work like most artists or their agents. It's more like every now and then he pops up somewhere, having created a piece that's either an embarrassing flop or a work of genius. From what I gather, there's never been anything mediocre about his work."

Barbara quoted some philosophy. "Heidegger said, 'He who thinks greatly must err greatly'.

Felicity asked Elsa, "What did you mean by successful in the art community?"

"I was thinking, 'successful' means noteworthy by critics, curated into international museums and supported by wealthy collectors."

Barbara clarified, "Definitions of art, or discussions of good is as it relates to art is a subject for aestheticians. In the fund-raising arm of the Institute, we avoid such subjects -- gladly!"

"Yes." Beverly said, "But how does the CAI make a decision before the work is made? At the point of presentation, there's no product, no work to pay for. Only a clay model."

Barbara interjected, "You've hit on an important issue that concerns me. Grants go to celebrated and secure artists. In most cases an award is based on the contemporary mode of the project, the reputation of the artist and continuity of the project with an established body of work. Mr. Alathon's work has few formal properties that could be called continuous and a reputation for, as Elsa said, erring greatly. According to Elsa, Michael and Theo, Philip may have a worthwhile funding opportunity but he's not acting as if he wants funding. While the institute may wish to support a venture on principle, in practice we have to be convinced of the artist's expertise, commitment and ability to create the work within a realistic time frame and budget. In any case, the screening process involves the artist's meeting with, say, Jeff Holmes. But we now know that, Philip refuses to meet. His work may 'speak for itself' in a language of pure excellence but the grant proposal has to be made in modern English by a person."

Then Beverly took the floor. "I've talked to people all over Summit County." She said. "Everybody will support it as long as it doesn't increase taxes. We'll have a budget for the estimated cost of construction, then for its perpetual maintenance, along with projections of income from the sale of postcards and memorabilia to tourists. Michael believes we could turn a profit. Meinstrom's makes a fortune on sales of that stuff."

"I'd think the support of the Summit County community could be the personal voice that speaks to the CAI concerns about need and commitment. I'm impressed with Beverly as the head of a new arts commission. That's a big step in the right direction. What we require is a projection of benefit that can be shared by the whole community. We need more than anecdotal evidence of interest or a restatement of Philip's philosophical ideals. If you have a bond election to establish an a local arts commission coming up, if that could be tied more explicitly to Philip's project it could give us some concrete event that represents democratic support."

Beverly spoke up quickly. "There's an event coming up. It's the Ullr Festival. If we could get a model of Mr. Alathon's sculpture on display in Breckenridge couldn't we just ask people what they think of it? What if we made a float for the Ullr Festival and let people see what we're talking about?"

"What a good idea." Felicity enthused. "The people who work on the float would all become a pep squad for the sculpture."

Michael was cautious. "It's not always wise to let people judge a work of art before they've had a chance to experience it over time. Remember how unpopular the Vietnam memorial was before it was built. Ross Perot started a political career with outraged pronouncements that the memorial would be an embarrassment and insult to the veterans. Now many people think it's the most important work of art in America. At first the people of Paris thought the Eiffel Tower was just a pile of iron junk and wanted it pulled down. Now it's the symbol of a nation. We have to be careful."

"I may be naive," Beverly said. "But I think at some point we have to trust people. Especially if we're asking them to pay for something and live with it the rest of their lives. We can ask them to trust us with their support but don't we have to show them what they're getting and help them understand it?"

"Philanthropy follows leadership." Barbara said and nodded in Beverly's direction. "The political climate will create the spirit within which the people will want to contribute."

The business of the meeting was tacitly adjourned and the remainder of the meal was savored along with pleasant conversation around the topics of New York style and Colorado scenery.

"Why don't we go visit Philip?" Michael asked Felicity after they finished eating. "You'll get a better perspective on everything when you see the model's progress".

"I didn't know he was that close. Do you mean he didn't have the time to join us in a meeting with a wealthy art patron and the representative of a distinguished art endowment but he'd have plenty of time for one of his buddies to drop in for a drink?"

Outside the cabin, Theo saw them approaching, dropped the armload of wood he'd just gathered for the night's fire pit, and rushed over with his greeting. "What are you doing over here? Philip's inside working away." He yelled to Philip "Michael and Fel are here. Switch off your genius and come on out."

It was the first time Felicity had seen Philip in years. She remembered him in a Tux at her wedding.

Now, here he was -- au natural. Jeans, flannel shirt, very long beard, but apparently in the peak of health.

Felicity took Philip's arm. "Come on. At least you can show me around."

As they strolled back into the cabin Michael and Theo unhurriedly started a fire in the fire pit. It was mid-afternoon. Fel fell in love with the model as soon as she saw it, while Philip explained what was left to do to finish it, some of which he didn't even know right now. Philip and Fel joined Theo and Michael around the nicely warming fire pit and the conversation turned to the work.

"So Philip" Felicity offered "you've dragged my husband to these mountains to help you with some flight of fantasy, huh? Caused him to desert his family, give up a chunk of his lucrative Manhattan law practice, and dream of making some sort of contribution to...to who knows what?"

"Is that what he called it -- flight of fantasy?"

"No, that's what I call it. Believe it or not, I've kept up with your career more than Michael. He's left the arts patronage to me. All I know about this venture is that my husband felt like he couldn't not do some ludicrous thing you've challenged him with."

"Ludicrous, huh?"

"Look, Philip, I'm just here to lend moral support to my husband's enterprises and, hopefully, to get in some raw love some time before I return to the real world. But what the hey? I support my dear husband in whatever he chooses to do to support me and the kids. ----- Oh, that's right. No fee for this one."

"Fel, when Michael married you, I told him the only thing I really adored about you was your sense of humor. Sure, he thought you were the most beautiful thing in the world. And while I appreciated his assessment, I couldn't identify with it 'cause, as you know, for me beauty is more than a well-tuned body or a set of mams.

"More to your point, the word 'fee' is one with which I'm only vaguely familiar. It would seem that your introduction of that word into our conversation lends credence to my initial estimation of you, that you have a sense of humor. Given your proclivity for tongue-in-cheek, dry directness, maybe you should be more aware of the cause Michael's directing his inestimable talents toward. By the way, at the expense of so-called 'client/attorney' relationships, to the best of my knowledge, Michael is here of his own free will. Theo. Did you coerce Michael?"

Theo shook his head.

"Cause?"

"'Cause' may be too strong a word. 'Cause' seems to denote an antithesis, a protagonist, if you will. But there probably isn't an 'anti' in this effort. I only want to contrapose beauty with a sort of Bachian sublimity if you'll excuse the mixed metaphor -- man-made beauty with natural beauty comparable with Bach's introduction of mathematics to sound -- and in so doing, elevate man."

"Come on Philip. Gimme a break. You're comparing yourself to Bach? What's this bullshit about sublimity and elevating man? When we were driving up here these mountains along the Continental Divide defy interpretation. You're telling me you're going to place some piece of plastic art amidst this scene and in so doing add something to the picture?"

"Your opinion of this project, in its directness, betrays a naivete that I guess needs resolving."

"YOU might have to resolve something, but I don't mind being naive. After all, I'm only looking after my husband's interests. I'd hate to see him make a fool of himself chasing a phantom."

"Phantom? Fel, you're mixing metaphors."

"Metaphor, schmetaphor. Let's get to the point. Your real concern here is to get free legal advice and perhaps some moral support for another of your whims. Am I right?"

Philip stood up, walked halfway around the fire-pit that formed the center of their being-there, folded his arms behind his back, and just stood there for a minute, collecting his thoughts.

In the background, as if trying to make an impression on Fel, one of those truly magnificent sunsets was bestowing its beauty on the four gathered there that evening in the opening. All the prismatic colors of the spectrum were there, daring to be appreciated behind cameoed mountain peaks off to the west. If ever thought could take place, if ever intuition and imagination could mingle, it would be in an atmosphere like this.

Philip allowed the moment to pass, but he wasn't going to lose his train of thought. He'd seen plenty of this scene before. Finally, he interjected unexpectedly, "The point, dear Felicity, is this. As a paradigm of rational thought, I have lived in and off these mountains you've been admiring for the last 24 hours, for years -- taking from them what they have to offer. In order of importance their offering has been Beauty, Bounty, Thought, Respect, Awe and Joy. As I move through these mountains, I opine that I'm not too unlike the others, whether turkeys from Texas passing through for skiing or elk hunting, or farmers/ranchers trying to eke a living out of these rocks and valleys, or fishermen trying to outsmart the rainbows, cutthroats and browns. If there's a difference, it's in the nature of the job to be done. I have mine, they have theirs. We, man, are under a natural imperative to treat this earth -- these mountains -- with respect, to give back in accordance with what we've taken. The native Indians know this well. Dame Fortune, relentless in natural justice, requires it. In a way, what we see is what they give us, through the filter of our imagination. And in a way, what they give us is what we require. What we see is what we give them. I'm going to give them something. From within my very being, I'm going to give to these mountains something they will appreciate (speaking metaphorically of course). And in so giving man's finitude among the magnanimity of nature's gift will provide a representation of a sort of natural ethic." Fel, mesmerized by Philip's ideation in such a setting could only reply "Dame Fortune's notion of natural justice needs more edification -- perhaps sometime later this evening or tomorrow or the next day."

Philip didn't even hear Felicity's off-hand comments. Instead, he began to describe his work, twirling and bending, reaching and stretching. He became so animated that Felicity could only sit there in awe. "This is the kind of genius the world needs" she thought, quite mesmerized.

****

After that visit with Philip and Theo, Felicity was ecstatic as she took a devilishly hot, steamy shower back at the cabin in Georgetown. Even as they arrived up at the tunnel, talk was scarce as they gazed at the potential location. The short drive down to Georgetown, was mostly in anticipation of arriving there.

At last, drenched by a warm, vaporous shower, she rubbed her lean body with fragrant soap, and massaged shampoo into her fine hair. Sure made her appreciate the small things in life.

Now that she was back, Felicity had a kind of consuming awareness she'd participated in something so unique, so eventful, that she knew she'd never forget it even if she couldn't fully explain it. She'd been caught up in the flow of a series of events in which she was both an observer and a participant. Although she felt its importance, she couldn't quite put her finger on the "for whom" -- the audience for which the stage had been set. In this respect, she wasn't unlike Philip.

No doubt, she'd been sold on the merit of Philip's project in a way she'd never been so convinced before, but the method, the manner of convincing remained an enigma. Philip had been compelling enough, but the idea -- the necessity of the project couldn't be escaped. She had been 'sucked into the web', not necessarily without her consent because she was open to it, but with a degree of willingness she didn't understand. The project wouldn't not happen if she had anything to do with it, which she now knew she would. Inexplicably, she felt helpless because she hadn't the slightest degree of choice. Christ, with Philip at the helm -- his charisma, his certitude, his foresight, his absolute genius -- who could doubt the success of his vision? Who could not be swept into helplessness by the consuming sense of necessity demanded by the project?

Whatever lingering doubts she'd had about Michael's involvement with Philip were not only completely dispelled, but she had a new sort of admiration for Michael -- for his confidence and resolve in taking on the job in the first place. Suddenly, she appreciated Michael's relationship to this consuming play. There was a time when she'd been jealous of Philip, when Michael placed him on, what seemed to be to Fel, a higher pedestal than her. But now, with an insight she'd never known before, she finally had a glimpse of the unique nature of the bond between them.

As she soaked in the shower, she was embarrassed by her own naiveté.

Nonetheless somewhere in some societal recesses of her embarrassingly immature mind, she could already envision cocktail parties in Manhattan which would include, if not Philip himself as honored guest, at least ample conversation about his work and her experiences with him.

Chapter Ten

"We are too late for the gods and too early for Being. Being's poem, just begun, is man." Heidegger, <u>Being and Time</u>

****

Beverly had returned to her work on the float committee with a renewed conviction that what she was doing for the art commission was important. Out of respect for Darcy's bad experiences with men Beverly didn't tell her that an appreciation of Philip's art could have an erotic dimension but why shouldn't love of art mean a particularly deep feeling for the artist even if from a distance.

With Andrew's help they had secured the use of an empty county garage as a workshop for construction of the float. Darlene had made the arrangements for the garage and stayed around to help clean up the space. Beverly and Darcy were surprised to hear that Darlene knew something about Philip Alathon's work. Darlene even thought she could get in touch with some art students who might be willing to help build the float.

Two days later Andrew dropped by the garage for a visit. He hadn't volunteered any actual work. Beverly greeted him with a kiss on the cheek. His smiling glance over to Darcy was met with an impenetrable stare that froze the curl on his lips and made him turn abruptly back to Beverly.

"You know," Andrew said, "I think the snow boarders are out in force this year. There's a bunch hanging around in town."

The snowboarders were always identifiable by their scruffy clothes and youthful swagger but the bunch Andrew was referring to was even darker and more chaotic in appearance than usual.

Andrew continued. "All the boys have full body tattoos as far I can see and the girls multiple body piercings."

One of Andrew's recent challenges in life was that he'd so far proven too old to date a woman with a nose ring. But there was always tomorrow.

"They usually keep to themselves," Beverly said, "and mostly out of the way."

"Except when they can't resist the temptation to hot dog at the expense of a conventional skier." Andrew couldn't resist the opportunity to correct Beverly.

The county had a zero tolerance policy about harassment of skiers. They were valuable customers who paid top dollar to look cool on the slopes. They were not to be shown up, offended or even slightly annoyed. This bunch on the street corners were acting as a unit. They were signaling and exchanging information. They appeared to be on some kind of a mission.

"I hope we're not faced with some new kind of organized snowboarder intrusion." Andrew said with conviction.

The bay door rattled and clanged open. The whole group of tattooed, black clad, body pierced, and newcomers swaggered youthfully from the snowblind street to the center of the garage. Little Darlene trailed behind them in her shapeless parka and overshoes.

"These are the art students." She said. "They've come to help with Mr. Alathon's float."

The Styrofoam and papier-mâché rendering of Dancing Star began to take shape. Every day, it became more like Philip's sketches and model. From a distance, it had the shape of an hourglass with a large bulge in the funnel. But up close, you could see, even in Beverly's crude replica, the beauty of the curves from any and all angles. The slight curves at the ankle and knees, the firm stomach, small breasts, and exact tilt of the head revealing the faintest Adams-apple, the tiny nose and eye cavity, on up to the delicate fingers. Any vertical cross section revealed the same outer form. When people asked who could have been the model Beverly replied that it was just some famous dancer.

Darlene's art students were diligent workers who, in spite of their anarchist appearance, took Beverly's instructions with a disarming ease. Willie's employees contributed their time willfully and without pay. They stuffed some 48 dozen cases of different colored Kleenex through chicken-wire until their hands were numb and Philip's vision emerged as a monolith with a huge green and white shaggy mountain in the background. The art students kept mostly to themselves and put in long hours, working on into the night after Beverly and the local volunteers had retired to dinners and warm beds. They looked to be exchanging information and enjoying their work in ways that was not shared with the other volunteers.

****

Ullr-Fest was its usual drunken, ribald, revelry. There were seventeen entrants in the parade. Six real floats, four bands, two groups of motorcyclists, the fire-department, the sheriff's department, and a few unaligned groups that stumbled into the parade accidentally.

Theo had come down to Breckenridge to join the festivities and get a first-hand impression of the impact the sculpture design would have on the citizenry. The Ullr-Fest might do more to promote Philip's project than $50,000 worth of marketing could do. Even without funds in the current fiscal budget Beverly's Arts department could begin a variety of fund-raising activities, and enter into negotiations for land easements, rights-of-way, leases and even purchases. Most importantly Barbara Simpson was in Breckenridge to observe the degree of community support that was growing up around Philip's proposal.

Philip, of course, stayed behind. Even at this late stage of the design he would be making adjustments to the form and would probably still be working on the sculpture down to the moment that the final mold was cast.

Darcy had straightened out the seams of Beverly's costume and given her a kiss for good luck as Meinstrom's float lurched into motion. After riding at Beverly's side for a few feet she jumped off as the float formed up with the rest of the parade. Theo and Barbara would be at the end of the parade route so she hurried down the block in their direction jostling a few revelers along the way.

Herr Meinstrom's float was without a doubt the grandest in the parade. Many observers might have held the opinion that the monolith and mountain paled compared to Beverly herself. She endured 20-degree weather in leotards, a ballet skirt and a form-revealing, white camisole, while the float's theme beckoned "Vote Yes for Referendum One". Two of the six float judges were county commissioners, and the resounding applause from the crowds lining Main Street as the Meinstrom float went by didn't go unnoticed. If adoration of Beverly's beauty seemed to be the overwhelming impetus for the crowd's reaction it was missed by the judges. By and large, they were all mostly drunk.

****

Theo and Barbara Simpson had found a spot out of the wind on the south end of the parade route. They were joined by several other temperate persons who were sober enough to still be feeling the weather. Beverly had picked up Barbara in Denver and introduced her to Darcy Rios-Doria. Darcy would help Beverly get the float moving and join them up the street to watch it go by.

The parade was still blocks away when a bearded man on the sidewalk lifted a Bible over his head heralded a summons for repentance. This kind of street life wasn't common or welcome in Breckenridge. Theo knew that some legal pretext would quickly be found to get him out of town.

"You'll know who they are." The man prophesied. "These are they who have come out of the great tribulation; they have washed their robes and made them white in the blood of the Lamb."

Remaining unrepentant, the prophet's audience of Ullr-festers looked up the street for the parade or up and down the sidewalk hoping to spot a cop who would move him out of the way.

"You'll hear the seven trumpets." At the mention of trumpets the man had Theo's attention.

"Count them down with me." The prophet commanded. "One: a third of the vegetation will be burned. Two: a mountain will fall into the sea and a third of the waters will be defiled. Three: A shooting star named Wormwood will turn a third of the fresh water sour."

Theo remembered that months ago in the camp up at Coon Hill someone had burned vegetables and turned some of the drinking water sour, and there had been had been a rockslide soon after. A third of the vegetables supplies were ruined, rocks fell and water soured. Was this really a coincidence? Theo had left a note that said "Wormwood." It couldn't be a coincidence.

"Trumpet number four:" The prophet continued. "A third of the light is extinguished." Theo remembered his missing Coleman lantern.

"Five: The key to the bottomless pit releases a swarm of terrible insects."

The picture of pits and bugs forced the conclusion. Mysterious events in camp were parallel to this man's ranting. But of course! Theo was astonished that he hadn't put this together before. Seven trumpets. Seven seals. A south Louisiana boy should know something about The Bible.

"What's the sixth trumpet?" Theo shouted.

As Darcy came up a few feet behind Theo she noticed a woman in an ill-defined heavy parka standing just behind and to the left of them. The woman was in the company of a distinctly colorful man with a bible in his hand. Darcy could see that the woman was subtly tugging and maneuvering the man so that they would be standing closer to Theo and Barbara.

The woman began speaking confidentially to her companion and Darcy listened. He was replying softly and couldn't really be heard but the woman's voice took on a muted tone that was still loud enough to be heard distinctly by everyone in her vicinity. She was standing right at Barbara Simpson's ear.

"Everybody's getting a good show this year." The woman said. "But what's the mystery about Meinstrom's entry? How did that Beverly girl get in charge of anything? ... That's not what I heard. ... I hope not. ... That boyfriend of hers turned out to be a real bastard and now she's got this other one. ... Michael Lovell who do you think? He put her up to this float and that's not all he got her up. ... Because I know things. He's got that sweet smile but he's had every whore in Georgetown since he started staying out here. ... That bartender who used to work over at the Gold Pan for one."

Darcy took a step toward the street and then let her eyes drift over her shoulder as if looking for someone in the crowd. Without any apparent purpose she brought her gaze right to the face of the woman who was talking behind her. It was Darlene.

"Then he screwed that friend of the Hollister's." Darlene continued. "Everybody was so impressed with that long legged aristocratic. If you want my opinion she was a special friend of the old man Hollister. They were all trash. But she stayed behind in

Breckenridge to entertain Michael Lovell. I saw them together. Then there was that skinny girl who's been working on Meinstrom's float. Not Beverly. The other one. He was having at least two of them. Maybe all of them."

In her business Darcy knew when she was being set up and this was one of those times. She knew that Darlene's story was false in at least three instances because she was three of the women involved. Darlene was talking so that Barbara Simpson could overhear her. She wanted to distract Barbara from the success of the parade. But Darlene's volunteers had done much of the work on the float. Suddenly it was all so obvious. Darlene didn't bring in people to help but to sabotage.

Darcy had matched wits with some of the worlds most clever and cruel operatives in the world and dumpy little Darlene had run a complicated disinformation scheme right under her nose without being detected. It was just so improbable. But there it was. Obvious enough once uncovered. Darlene had been at the center of all the communications between Philip Alathon and the citizens of Summit County. Anyone who could help him had been thwarted, discredited, or humiliated. "Who knows?" she thought, "Maybe he's involved, too."

The parade was passing by in front. Beverly was smiling and waving. Watching parades on television she had never realized how hard it was to keep arms and hands in the air for such a long time but she was energized by the enthusiasm of the crowd. The front of Meinstrom's, where Theo and Barbara were watching was coming up. Beverly shifted her weight back and forth, alternated arms and soldiered on.

As Beverly waved to Barbara she began to notice a change on the faces of the people waving back. Their smiles were turning to curiosity and then alarm. They were looking past her at the model of the sculpture. She turned to see for herself. A purplish red fluid was gushing from between the legs of the papier-mâché woman. It was puddling like blood on the platform at Beverly's feet. In front of Beverly's startled eyes the skin of the statue broke apart and fragments scattered along the roadway.

A replica of a giant vagina was concealed in the wire mesh. Its center was glowing pink and surmounted by a curly black wire that bobbed in the wind. A powerful fan began to blow sticky wads of unrecognizable matter drenched in the red stuff all over the crowd. A big clump of matter that could have been the guts of a pig, but lighter and more propulsive, struck

Barbara Simpson's left shoulder.

Darcy seized Darlene from behind. "What have you done?" Darcy demanded.

The shock of discovery enraged Darlene. "Whore of Babylon!" She shouted. "Leave the dead alone. Blessed are the dead who die in the Lord henceforth. Blessed indeed, says the spirit, that they may rest from their labors, for their deeds follow them."

Darcy's instincts about recent events was now so clear. She couldn't imagine how she had been in the dark for so long. Darcy had collected loose fragments of the history of Summit County and they came together in an instant. "Where is your husband?" She demanded.

"Buried!" Darlene screamed. "And this whore won't dig him up."

"Is your husband's body is buried on the site proposed for Alathon's sculpture."

"I killed him for the whore monger that he was and I've kept him there all of these years."

Theo was helping Barbara Simpson wipe off as much of the bloody mess as he could.

"She hid her husband's body at the excavation site when the Eisenhower Tunnel was under construction." Darcy explained.

"And what's the sixth trumpet?" Theo shouted.

"Angels of the four rivers kill a third of mankind." Darlene raged. "Put in your sickle and reap, for the hour to reap has come for the harvest of the earth is fully ripe."

Darcy turned to Theo. "I don't know how many people are involved in this. You've got to stay with Beverly." She insisted. "Philip Alathon is in certain danger. I'll try to help him."

Darcy knew that the long walk away from the Ullr-Fest and a twenty minute drive up to Silverthorne would be too late to help Philip but she had to try.

****

As Darcy entered, the cabin at Silverthorne filled with a terrifying silence. A quick search out back revealed Philip Alathon sitting on the edge of a snow bank just beyond the fire pit. A body was sprawled on a bloody patch of snow beside him. It was lying on its back dressed in a white robe. A crown with twelve pointed stars had fallen from its head and was resting on the ground nearby. Most incongruously, two half-moon shapes constructed from a metal alloy were attached to the toes of its boots.

"Are you alright?" Darcy knelt between Philip and the body.

"I suppose so. He was coming up behind me with a knife. Someone killed him with a single shot from somewhere over beyond the property line."

Darcy looked back up in the direction of the shooter. "What a shot! I could find that guy a job."

"The corpse has two shiny things attached to his boots," Philip said.

"She's a woman with a crown of twelve stars and the moon under her feet. The woman clothed in the sun from the Apocalypse of John in Revelations."

"She's actually Lem," Philip said, "from the hunting lodge back in Montana."

"Yes I know. He's Darlene's brother. He and Darlene killed her husband twenty years ago."

"How do you know?"

"She admitted the murder and I put other pieces together. I've been trying to keep an eye on your project but I've failed at almost every turn. I think Hugh has been watching out for you up here and killed Lem when he knew you were in real danger."

"Is T-Boy all right?"

"Yes."

"And who are you?"

"I represent people who would like to see your proposed sculpture built, the owners of the land at the tunnel."

"And why?"

"Because they want the place to be undisturbed for now. The creation of an important cultural site would secure this location on into the indefinite future. I've botched this so badly that I'll do everything I can to get them to help you get use of the land and probably some funding. But you'll have to understand your situation. It would be dangerous for you to attempt to discover who they are. Let me tell you this much. Zhou Enlai, Premier of China was once asked by an enthusiastic young journalist what he thought of the French Revolution. Zhou replied, "It's too soon to tell. For some cultures a two-hundred-year time frame is short term planning."

Philip and Darcy drove over to Silverthorne and reported to the police. A coroner was sent to retrieve Lem's body. The story Philip and Darcy told wasn't at all convincing to the chief of police. Darlene and Lem were insane killers and some unknown marksman had saved Philip's life. Darcy would not implicate Hugh based on her assumptions even it meant taking herself off the hook. Without witnesses to the contrary Darcy who could convince any man of anything was released from custody and Philip who was by nature a suspicious character and uncooperative was retained for further questioning.

Darcy returned to Breckenridge to see if she could salvage any kind of relationship with Barbara Simpson. Darcy found Theo and Barbara at Beverly's house having some hot cocoa and Peppermint Schnapps. Beverly introduced Darcy. Barbara was still shaken but regained some sense of composure as Darcy told of events with Lem and Philip in Silverthorne. Darcy was at her profession best convincing, comforting and reassuring an angry woman who was accustomed to privilege, deference and respect but had just been splashed with pig blood and involved in a murder. Darcy continued with what she knew about Darlene and the imposter art students' role in the float disaster. Barbara was returning to New York tomorrow but assured Beverly and Theo that she would keep Philip's grant proposal open and wait until the police reports and outcome of any legal action before making a decision.

It would be some time before Philip ceased to be the prime suspect in Lem's murder but deranged Darlene eventually confessed everything with apocalyptic enthusiasm. With the help of a backhoe the body of Darlene's husband was uncovered under a recent landslide but exactly where she said it was buried twenty years ago.

****

In the weeks following the dismissal of charges against Philip, Barbara returned to consideration of Philip's proposal as chair of the Arts Advisory Committee. Theo sent new photos and cost estimates to New York for preliminary presentation to present the board. Barbara wrote to Beverly that she was ready to push the project forward but wanted them to be cautious and get their feet on some firm new ground.

"I'll meet Philip and see the model first."

Barbara returned to Breckenridge with the assurance that she wouldn't be invited to any more parades. Theo and Beverly reintroduced her to Darcy who was anxious to relate her involvement with the project, vis-à-vis the tunnel land.

"I'm sure my clients are going to be willing to front some of the funds for the construction of the infrastructure of Dancing Star, and probably provide an endowment for its upkeep and maintenance. More money will be needed for the foundry work, engineering, insurance, permits and the like. It's highly unlikely that the county will provide any funds. We were encouraged by your organization's interest. The western world's opinion that New York is the only place that art is produced is not shared by my clients. I can't reveal much about them now but they definitely think the center of the world should be shifting more toward the Pacific. Colorado is a step in the right direction."

"Since the murder and investigation Philip has never been better known." Beverly said cautiously. "Isn't all publicity good publicity?"

"You may be right about that," Barbara replied after taking time to recollect discussions over dinner and drinks in New York. "Philip's reputation has always been helpful in some circles while damaging in others. The international interest in Philip's predicaments has cut both ways. Any news of a bizarre criminal investigation involving a controversial artist with murder and evangelical fury in Colorado will trend in the media. We have the world's attention but need to return to specifics of the project. When I thought Philip might be going to prison I thought I'd know where he was when I wanted a meeting with him."

Theo broke in "I think I can make that happen."

After they disbursed Theo headed to Silverthorne and Darcy gave Barry Hollister a call in Connecticut. After bringing Barry up to date on the events of the last few days she almost demanded "Barry, you've got to keep your family behind this project. Your Dad knows Elsa, and Elsa has influence over Barbara Simpson. I think Barbara will need a little help getting this project agreed upon by her committee."

"I'll do what I can."

Theo headed up to Casper, Wyoming for a quick, preliminary meeting with Charlie Bird, owner of CW Bronze Works. CW had an excellent reputation for producing high quality bronze work for almost any conceivable use. Theo had photos of Philip's model, along with sketches. When he entered Charlie's office, he saw a former rodeo bull rider. Charlie was your typical cowboy. Boots, large silver and bronze belt buckle, jeans, western shirt complete with pearl snap buttons. His hat was on his desk along with what appeared to be several blueprints. Charlie had worked with Philip on another project 5-6 years ago, one of Philip's projects that was a complete flop in Santa Barbara.

After Theo introduced himself Charlie said "So how's the wild and crazy man doing these days?"

Theo told him about Philip's bout with blindness, then got right to the point. We're hoping to construct a large, seventy foot tall sculpture at the western portal of Eisenhower tunnel. Are you familiar with it?"

"Yeah, been through there several times on my way to the Roaring Fork and Frying Pan rivers near Aspen. Some great fishing and huge fish in those rivers, maybe not as big as in the Big Horn, but much more fun – and difficult to catch, and you're not confined to a drift boat. Ever been there?"

"No. Well I've been to Aspen. But I'm not much of a fisherman – or angler."

"Too bad. You've missed out on one of life's great pleasures. Anyway, how can I help ol' Philip?"

"Take a look at these photos and sketches. Can you transform something like this into a seventy foot sculpture?"

After examining the photos and sketches for a few minutes, Charlie said "Assuredly it can be done. There's plenty of copper in these parts, so getting the material is no problem. It would be hollow, made in probably three sections for the body, and some smaller sections for the fine detail. Support would come from a central H beam sunk into several feet of concrete. The key to the whole process is the model. The quality and detail of the final product is totally dependent on the quality and detail of the model. I have all the equipment needed to translate and digitize the model into the proper size molds. I would also suggest that you let me hire and oversee the project from start to finish as I know the right personnel for the job."

"What about cost? And time?"

"Time first. Given that there's barely a four month window of building time at twelve thousand feet, and that it will take the better part of nine months to get the molding done and transported to the location, you're looking at a minimum of two years, once I have the get go. As for cost, factoring in materials, engineering fees, labor, oversight and profit, two to two and a half million is a rough estimate. Until we have things like soil samples, possible wind gradient analysis, earthquake and traffic vibration, it's hard to nail down a firm estimate. In fact, if I were to take the job, I'd probably want a cost-plus-materials-plus-profit, with a not-to-exceed type of contract. What is your time-frame, by the way?"

"It's hard to nail down anything specific. My best guess is that it will take several months to get all the loose ends tied up and give you the 'get go'."

"Just keep me in the loop. I have plenty of projects and will need some forewarning to get this project planned and scheduled. It will require hiring some additional, temporary staff as well."

"Well, I have enough info to, as they say, 'make me dangerous'. We'll get back to you as things progress."

"Give a big 'howdy-do' and slap on the back to Philip for me."

"Will do."

Theo headed back to Summit County wondering just what the next steps would be. All the players Michael, Darcy, Barbara, Beverly and Philip—and perhaps even Andrew Wolltrip -- needed to get on the same page somehow. And he needed to get Barbara and Philip together.

Surprisingly, Philip had started fire in the fire pit, and was standing with his back to the flames when Theo drove into the driveway.

"Whatcha doing out here?"

"For whatever reason, this afternoon I was remembering all those insightful times up at Granite in Wyoming, so I thought I'd see if I could, at least partially, replicate the with the help of a campfire."

"Those were some memorable times, for sure. Any insightful results?"

"No, not really. The surroundings here just aren't as conducive to stirring up the imagination. And there's this new focus."

"My meeting with Charlie Bird went well, and he sends 'the crazy man' his kind regards."

"Charlie can be quite the character when he's had a few shots of Wild Turkey. Can you imagine riding a one-ton, bucking bull around just for the thrill of competition? I'm glad he gave it up before he got seriously maimed or killed. He's one of the best bronze craftsmen in the world."

"Look, Philip. I hate to change the subject, but what may well be the most important meeting you've ever not wanted to have needs to happen tomorrow. Barbara Simpson is in Breckenridge hoping to learn about your project. She is the chair of New York's Community Arts Initiative's Artist Advisory Committee, and she has great influence over any funding the Initiative doles out. And we need funding."

Theo related the essence of his conversation with Charlie Bird yesterday.

"If we're talking two to three million, we're going to need all the help we can get. I know you don't like dealing with this sort of 'minutia', but it will be critical if you want Dancing Star to reach Fruition."

"Bring 'er on."

Knowing that Philip loved looking at Beverly, he called her and asked her to bring Barbara over around mid-morning tomorrow. In the mean-time, he tidied up the cabin as best he could, and helped Philip get the model ready for a methodical viewing.

Prior to their arrival, Theo did his best to keep Philip in a good mood, joking about some of the great fun they'd had over the years, camping, thinking and discussing. When he heard Beverly's car pull into the drive, he went to the door. "Welcome to our humble abode and art shop." Philip was doing his best to keep his eyes off Beverly.

"Barbara Simpson meet Philip Alathon."

"How singularly pleasant to finally come face-to-face with someone whose work I've followed for years. And under such 'interesting' circumstances given the parade events, Charlene, Lem. But you're used to controversy aren't you Mr. Alathon."

"I can't remember the last time I was called "Mr. Alathon" – probably by some justice or another. So please call me Philip, and if it's OK, I'll call you Barbara."

"Please do. Now why not show me what you've got and tell me what you can about it."

They walked over to the work area, and Philip removed the sheet from his clay model and began "This piece is called 'Dancing Star'".

"In <u>Zarathustra,</u> Nietzsche said 'one must still have chaos in oneself to give birth to a dancing star'. Some Greek Pre-Socratic, I forget which one now, said "All the world was chaos, then MIND arose and made order". Bringing order out of chaos is also a theme in among many religions. No doubt my life has seen its elements of chaos. But this sculpture is not an egotistical attempt to bring order to a natural backdrop that is already sublimely ordered beyond anything man could contribute, but rather an attempt to show man's genius as a part of the natural state of Being."

After spending about ten minutes walking around the model, pausing, bending down for different perspectives, but not touching it, Barbara told Philip "the piece is quite striking, and, yes, I can see elements of a ballerina throughout. When I envision it at the Eisenhower Tunnel I imagine it could garnish that space very fascinatingly. So, Philip, I'm convinced and I will present Dancing Star to my Board of Directors for funding as soon as I get some details about the potential cost."

Everybody breathed a big sigh of relief.

"Thank you, Barbara. Theo and Darcy can provide those details. If I had some Champagne and enough glasses, I'd offer a toast."

"Perhaps next time and it's a bit early for me anyway. For now, I need to get back and finalize my travel arrangements back home."

With that, Barbara and Beverly left. As soon as Theo heard the car exit the driveway, he, uncharacteristically, gave Philip a high five and said "now if I can just get everybody together and on the same page."

Chapter Eleven

"We should never allow our fears or the expectations of others to set the frontiers of our destiny" - Heidegger

****

Theo called Michael in a very good mood. "Hey Pal, Barbara just left and, guess what, she's going to recommend the project to her Board."

That's great, and it appears the referendum passed by a pretty substantial margin, without any funding, however."

Theo described his discussion with Charlie Bird then said "Now we need to get all the loose ends tied up."

Michael set to work on the decisive meeting. He called Andrew first to solicit his help in getting the county officials together. That would bring in Lawrence Richgood, chairman of the Board of County Commissioners and James Bagnold, head of engineering for the Road and Bridge department. Andrew agreed to help, primarily because it would be a further opportunity to mingle with Beverly and try to figure out Darcy.

Then, Michael called Beverly and Darcy, who enthusiastically agreed.

Michael holed up in Georgetown for the next few days and got down to, what he thought, sadly, might be end to his participation in the project. The best thing a lawyer can do for a client is to make himself unnecessary.

The meeting was in the County Commons a week later. Absent again, to everyone's chagrin was Phillip. Theo apologized again that Phillip had some finishing touches to put on the model.

Michael called the meeting to order, and briefed everyone on the status to date. Next, Theo described his visit with Charlie Bird and focused on the two to three million dollar price tag. Then Darcy offered that her client was, 'as we speak', preparing a lease for the land, but didn't know who to name as the lessee. Michael interjected that this meeting should answer that question. Darcy also said that her client was donating one million dollars for the construction and guaranteeing one hundred thousand dollars annually for maintenance and upkeep. Michael said that they could reasonably expect to get one to one-point-three million from Barbara's group.

"So now, there are still a few issues to resolve. First, I suggest we form a board only, nonprofit organization (NPO) called the Tunnel Art Committee, and I have prepared all the documents, both state and federal that we need. The board members would be the people at this meeting. Any decisions needing to be made by the board would require majority approval. I suggest Lawrence should be President, and Andrew should be Secretary/Treasurer. Both their signatures would be required on disbursement checks. A bank account would be set up at Alpine Bank. Construction would be totally in Charlie Bird's hands, but James, as the head county engineer, would perform inspections as he deemed necessary. His design approval would be required before any funds could be disbursed. Finally, in her position as head of the county Arts Initiative, Beverly would be charged with raising the additional two- to five-hundred thousand dollars needed to meet the funds match requirement required by the Community Arts Commission. She would have your support, as well as the majority of the county population as demonstrated by their support of the referendum.

"That's the guts of what's needed. Now, any discussion?"

James asked pointedly, "Are we to perform our functions without pay?"

Michael responded "Yes. Unless you desire to increase the ultimate cost of the project, board members will serve gratis. Oversight of the property on behalf of the county will be included in the commissioner's stipend."

"Pitiful as it is," James smiled.

Lawrence interjected "Consider it part of the cost of living in and even creating, paradise."

James then asked "What about on-going maintenance?"

"Good question, James. The generous provision of annual maintenance funds from Darcy's client will be used for such things as periodic policing and removal of trash and debris from the property. An annual high pressure, steam cleaning of the entire sculpture will rid it of soot and muck generated by the huge volume of traffic up there."

Andrew asked "In that case what's holding this up. When is ground-breaking?"

"That's an uncertainty right now. First we have to get Charlie Bird and his engineer involved to design the substructure. With James' help soil samples, wind and earthquake analysis will set redundant structural standards for safety and serviceability."

Darcy finally stood up and said, "Even though there are many details yet to work out, I have no doubt that this experience and diverse body can cope with them. I therefore make a motion that we approve Michael's program and move forward with confidence and build a majestic testament to the quality of life in this county."

Beverly seconded the motion, and the agreement was unanimous.

Theo related the events of the meeting to Philip when he got back to the cabin. "I guess we need to get the model up to Charlie Bird."

"I'm as ready as I'll ever be."

En route home the next day, after delivering the model to Charlie, Phillip asked Theo "Wonder what I'll do next?"

Made in the USA
Charleston, SC
09 July 2016